UNEXPECTED TROUBLE!

Benjamin Franklin stepped forward and shook hands with them all. "Goodbye to you, and God speed," he smiled.

When he had gone, the Professor turned to the chronocycle. He reached for the switches. And then he paused, with his hand in midair.

"Goodness gracious!" he said. "There's one thing I had completely forgotten."

"What is it?" said Danny.

The Professor's face had become very pale. "I hadn't thought how to get us back to the right day of our own, exact time," he said. "I haven't any way of knowing precisely when to stop the machine so that we will return to the day we left."

Danny Dunn, Time Traveler

**Jay Williams and
Raymond Abrashkin**

Illustrated by Owen Kampen

AN ARCHWAY PAPERBACK
Published by POCKET BOOKS • NEW YORK

An Archway Paperback published by
POCKET BOOKS, a Simon & Schuster division of
GULF & WESTERN CORPORATION
1230 Avenue of the Americas, New York, N.Y. 10020

Published by arrangement with McGraw-Hill, Inc.
Library of Congress Catalog Card Number: 63-18545

ISBN: 0-671-43680-5

First Pocket Books printing May, 1979

10 9 8 7 6 5 4 3

AN ARCHWAY PAPERBACK and colophon are
trademarks of Simon & Schuster.

Printed in the U.S.A.

IL 4+

Contents

1. The Locked Door   1
2. The Professor Surrenders   11
3. The Chronocycle   21
4. An Unexpected Visitor   33
5. Possible Joe   41
6. Father Abraham's Almanack   48
7. Captives of the Clevelands   56
8. Stranded in the Past   68
9. Breakfast and a Discovery   76
10. A Walk in Yesterday   86
11. The Red Lion Inn   101
12. An Oversight   111
13. The Long Count   117
14. Joe Possible   130

1
The Locked Door

Mrs. Dunn, like all mothers, had a magical ear. She could hear her son Danny grumbling on the other side of a solid wall; she could hear him *not* getting up in the morning; once in a while she could even hear him thinking.

On this particular sunny April afternoon, as she did her ironing in the kitchen, she heard a series of noises which would have puzzled or startled a stranger but which she understood at once. First there was a CRASH which shook the house. Then a scuffling sound. Then a series of thuds. Then a low growling which grew louder and which finally became Danny himself, in the kitchen doorway.

He ran a hand through his coppery red hair, and said glumly, "H'lo, Mom."

Mrs. Dunn eyed her son's freckled face. Usually, it was rosy and cheerful, but today his lips drooped and his blue eyes were clouded.

She said, "There are some fresh butter-scotch-nut cookies in the pantry. They'll cheer you up. I'm sure you'll pass the history test without any trouble. After all, this is Friday; you've got the whole weekend for studying."

Danny stared at his mother with admiration. "Gosh, Mom, you're fantastic," he said. "How do you do it? How'd you know I have a history test on Monday?"

"It's very simple," his mother replied, deftly ironing a shirt collar. "But I'm not sure I ought to give away motherly secrets. First, you slammed the front door behind you. I knew at once that something was bothering you. You dragged your feet over to the hall table and dumped your schoolbooks on it one at a time. Then I knew it had something to do with school, because you only bring home lots of books when you have weekend homework to do. Next, I heard you mumble, 'Rats! First Continental Congress. Second Continental Congress. Rats, rats, rats!' That told me the rest of the tale."

Danny laughed. "Pretty smooth," he said. Then his face grew gloomy once more. "Darn old history anyway," he said. "I hate that subject. Why do they have to teach it?"

"Better hurry up and get yourself a couple of cookies," his mother advised. "You sound to me as though your brain is giving way. How could you be educated without knowing something about the history of the human race?"

Danny dug into the crock in the pantry and brought out two large, soft, still-warm cookies. He poured himself a glass of milk and sat down at the kitchen table.

"Mmm," he said, dreamily. "I love the smell of fresh cookies and the smell of fresh ironing. I guess you're right. We do have to learn some history. But it's so dull—all those names and dates."

"Funny," said Mrs. Dunn, sprinkling a little water over another shirt. "When I was a girl I used to think the same thing about mathematics. All those numbers—!"

"But that's different," Danny protested. "Math is fun. It's almost as much fun as physics, or electronics."

Mrs. Dunn chuckled, pressing the hot iron into the shirt sleeves. "It's all a matter of taste," she said.

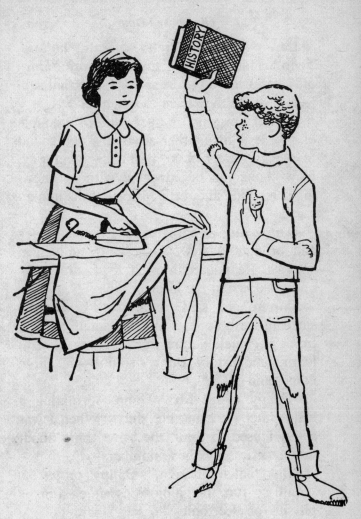

"But it's so dull—all those names and dates."

Danny shook his head. "No," he replied, "science is *real*. And all that history stuff is dead and gone. That's why it's not interesting."

"You talk it over with Professor Bullfinch," said Mrs. Dunn, with a smile. "I'm sure he doesn't feel that way."

Danny's father had died when Dan was only a baby, and Mrs. Dunn, to support herself, had taken the job of housekeeper to the famous scientist Euclid Bullfinch. Although Professor Bullfinch devoted part of his time to teaching at Midston University, he was able to do a considerable amount of private research and had his own well-equipped laboratory built onto the back of his house. He had grown very fond of Danny and had taught him a great deal about science. Between the boy and the kindly, thoughtful man a deep affection, almost like that of father and son, had grown up over the years.

Danny rested his elbows on the table and leaned forward. "Is the Professor still locked in his laboratory?" he asked, in a low voice.

Mrs. Dunn nodded. "He came out for a few minutes this morning and had some coffee, but I haven't seen him all the rest of the day. I brought him some lunch and he told me to leave it outside the door. He never touched it."

"It isn't like him to be so secretive," Danny mused. "He usually tells us what he's working on."

"I don't think he's being secretive," said Mrs. Dunn, folding up the last of her ironing. "It's just that he's working so hard on this new project, I think he's forgotten everything else."

She put her hand gently on her son's shoulder. "I'm sure he'll tell you about it when he's ready," she said. "Meanwhile, you'd better start preparing for that test."

"Yes, yes, that's what I'm doing," said the Professor's voice. He had wandered into the room and stood beaming rather vacantly at them.

"I was looking for a cup of coffee," he said. "You left some lunch for me outside the lab door, but the coffee was cold. Really, Mrs. Dunn, I'm surprised at you. Ice-cold coffee—?"

She put her hands on her hips and frowned at him. "Euclid Bullfinch," she said, sternly, "that tray was left outside your door over four hours ago."

"It was? Dear me. I thought it was only a few minutes since you knocked."

He turned to go. Mrs. Dunn said, "Don't you want that coffee?"

Professor Bullfinch passed a hand over his eyes. "I'm sorry," he said. "I'm afraid I'm rather scatterbrained today."

Generally, the Professor was anything but absent-minded. A jolly, plump man with a round, mild face, he usually had a bright, alert look. But now it was clear something was absorbing all his concentration.

He took the coffee Mrs. Dunn handed him and began to stir it, although he had not yet put any sugar or cream into it. Still stirring, he said, "I didn't realize you knew I was nearly ready to test my apparatus."

"It was Danny's test we were talking about," said Mrs. Dunn.

"Oh, really? What are you testing, Dan?"

"I'm not testing anything, Professor," Danny replied. "I'm going to *be* tested."

"Heavens! Are you part of an experiment?"

Danny burst out laughing. "It's history test. In school."

"Yes, and he's complaining that history is dull," said Mrs. Dunn. "He thinks because something happened a few hundred years ago, it isn't real."

"Isn't real? Bless my soul," said the Professor, still stirring away busily at his cup. Suddenly, he realized what he was doing, and stopped. "My dear boy, the past is right here, all around us. This very house is full of the past. It was built in 1750 for a gentleman named Jonathan Turner. Haven't you ever noticed the initials 'J.T.' branded in the huge, square beam over the fireplace? Those are his initials, probably put there with a hot poker by his own hand."

"Yes, I know, that's all very interesting," said Danny, with a shrug. "But you can't see the past—it's over with. I like science because it's what's happening right now."

The Professor dipped a finger into his coffee and tasted it thoughtfully. "Hmm. So you think the past has vanished, do you?" he said. "Let me ask you something. You're interested in astronomy, aren't you?"

"Well, sure. You know I built that three-inch telescope with you, last year."

"And you looked through it at Sirius, the Dog Star, the brightest star in the heavens. Do you remember how far away it is?"

"Eight and eight-tenths light years," Danny said, promptly. "Fifty-one trillion miles."

"Exactly. The light from Sirius took nearly nine years to get here, didn't it? So the star you saw was not the star as it was when you looked at it, but the star of nearly nine years before. You were looking right smack at the past."

Danny blinked. "Gee, that's right," he said. "I never thought of that."

"Yes," the Professor went on, with a far-away look in his eyes, "how strange and magical discovery can be—better than a fairy tale! Remember the seven-league boots in the old stories? Today, you can have breakfast in London, get on a jet plane, and have lunch in New York. Want to grow tiny? Look through a microscope! Want to talk to someone on the other side of the earth? You can do it in five minutes! We've had to change all our ways of thinking, all our old ideas. For instance—what's the shortest distance between two points?"

"A straight line," Danny said, automatically.

"Not at all," cried the Professor. "Look at a globe of the earth. The shortest distance between London and New York is a curved line, over the earth's surface, as a plane flies. We're living in an age of magic, my boy, where time and space have to be looked at with new eyes."

He picked up his coffee cup and sipped at it. "Cold!" he said. "Heavens, I just can't seem to get a hot cup of coffee."

"If you'll wait a minute," Mrs. Dunn began.

"Not now," said the Professor. "I must get back to work. You can bring me some sandwiches and coffee in a few minutes—an hour or so—"

He strode out of the room.

"Wait, Professor Bullfinch!" Danny called. "I wanted to ask you about your own test."

He jumped to his feet and hurried after the scientist, but he was too late. He ran down the hall and got to the laboraory annex just as the door closed in his face. As he stood there hesitating, wondering whether to knock, he heard the sharp and positive *click* of the key turning in the lock as if the Professor had clearly said, "No admittance."

2
The Professor
Surrenders

Studying alone for a test is almost as hard as ditch-digging. But studying with friends can be as good as a party. There's only one hitch: you have to keep your mind on your work. And puzzling over the Professor's secret made this the one thing Danny couldn't do.

Saturday morning, he met with his two closest friends, Irene Miller and Joe Pearson, for a session on American history. They met at Irene's house, next door to Danny's. Irene, whose father was a professor of astronomy at Midston University, was as deeply interested in science as Danny and planned to become a physicist when she grew up. Joe, on the other hand, wanted to be a writer and was notori-

11

ous in school for his poems, made up to suit every occasion. The three settled down with their books in Irene's room and started work, but Danny couldn't keep his eyes away from the bay window. It faced the back yard, and sitting in the window seat, Dan could just see the corner of the Professor's laboratory jutting from the rear of his own house next door.

At last, he put down his book with a sigh. "If only I could find out what he's doing inside there," he said.

Joe stretched out his lanky body in the armchair, and put his open history book on top of his head. "Maybe some of these names and dates will soak down into my mind this way," he said, sadly. "We're not going to get much studying done if you keep worrying about the Professor."

"I'm not worrying about him," said Danny. "I'm just curious."

"Uh-huh. And every time you get curious, I get into trouble," Joe moaned. "Like the time you were curious about what would happen if you made an air conditioner out of some ice cubes and my mother's vacuum cleaner. *I* was the one who had to clean up the mess and dry out the vacuum cleaner."

"I'm sorry about that, Joe," said Danny. "But it did blow cold air, didn't it?"

"Oh sure. Only it would have been better in July, instead of January," Joe mumbled. He pulled the book down over his face like a tent. "Let's see . . . First Continental Congress was held in Philadelphia on September 74. . . . "

Irene giggled. "I think there's something wrong with that date, Joe," she said. She knelt in the window seat next to Dan and looked down into his back yard. "I wonder why the Professor hasn't told you anything,"

13

she said. "Could it be some kind of top secret work for the government?"

"I doubt it. We'd have had all sorts of generals and FBI men around. No, I think he'd tell me what it is if I had a chance to ask him. But you see, he only comes out of the lab for a few minutes at a time and then he's so deep in thought that he doesn't seem to pay much attention to what I say."

Danny stared at him. "Look in the window?" Joe suggested. "I wonder if I could make up a poem about this history? What rhymes with 'congress'?"

Danny stared at him. "Look in the window?" he repeated, slowly. "Maybe you've got something."

"I haven't got a rhyme for 'congress,' " Joe said, shaking his head.

Irene looked worried. "But Danny," she said, "I don't think the Professor would like that."

Danny ran his fingers through his hair. "I'll tell you what I think," he said. "I think Professor Bullfinch keeps the lab door locked because he doesn't want to be disturbed. But I'm sure he wouldn't mind my just *looking*. The thing is, it would be disturbing him if I went and stuck my head up against the window. So maybe if I could figure out a way of looking that wouldn't really *disturb* him. . . . "

He jumped up. "Hey, let's go down into your back yard for a minute, Irene," he said. "I've got an idea."

"Good-bye, good old First Continental Congress," Joe said. "Here comes trouble."

They ran down the stairs and out into Irene's yard. A high lilac hedge separated it from Danny's yard, and at the far end the lawns gave place to a pleasant little wood of birches and maples, now just leafing out in the fresh green of spring. Danny went round the lilacs and through the wood to a spot near a thick, ancient maple where the youngsters had once built a treehouse. From here, they could clearly see the back of Danny's house.

"Look," he said. "The window of our guest bedroom is up there. If I could make a long periscope and lower it from that window, I could just see into the end window of the laboratory."

"A periscope? How would you make such a thing?" asked Irene. "You need a pair of prisms to start with."

"Right." Danny's face was glowing with the excitement he felt when he was involved in a new project, and he carried his friends along with him so that they generally forgot everything else. "You've got an old pair of field glasses, Irene. They have prisms in them. Go get 'em. I'll be able to take them apart easily and put them together again—I did it with a pair of my mother's bird-watching glasses once."

Irene scampered off.

Joe said, "What else do you need?" A periscope sounds like a complicated kind of thing. Do you need a submarine to go with it?"

"No, it's simple. Just two prisms mounted at each end of a long tube. I think I can use some old copper pipe we have in the garage." Danny frowned, pensively. "It'll have to be pretty long, though. We'll have to measure the distance from the window to the ground."

"Now, listen," Joe protested. "If you think I'm going to climb up the side of your house with a ruler—"

"No, there's an easier way. And it's very interesting, too. I'll show you."

Danny took out his pocketknife and after searching about found a straight, thin sapling. He cut it off near the ground and trimmed the twigs from it.

"My hand span, from the tip of the thumb to the tip of the little finger when my fingers are stretched out, is exactly six inches," he said. "I measured it once so I'd never need to carry a ruler with me. So now I'll make this stick four spans long—just two feet."

He cut it off and led Joe out of the shadows of the trees onto the lawn. He stood the stick on end and asked Joe to hold it upright. Then he knelt down and in the same way measured its shadow.

"Aha!" he cried. "A two-foot stick throws a three-foot shadow."

"Fine. Congratulations," said Joe. "I'm sure this is a great discovery, but I don't get it."

"Now we measure the shadow of the house," said Danny. He ran to the corner of the house and, on his knees, began spanning the edge of the long shadow cast across the grass.

Irene ducked through the lilacs with the field glasses in her hand. She gaped at Dan and said, "What on earth are you looking for?"

"Sh!" said Joe. "Don't interrupt him. He's measuring shadows."

Irene stared at him, and he stared back. Then he raised his eyebrows and shrugged. "You're right," he said. "It does sound kind of nutty, doesn't it?"

"Thirty feet," Danny said triumphantly, standing erect.

"Listen, Dan," said Irene, as they went back to the edge of the woods. "I was just thinking—"

"Wait a sec." He flapped a hand at her. "A three-foot shadow comes from a two-foot stick. So a thirty-foot shadow would come from a twenty-foot house. Right?"

"Right," said Irene. "But listen—"

"I measured the shadow to the edge of the eaves. That's where the top of the guest-room window comes. Now we subtract the distance from the ground to the sill of the laboratory window. About five feet. So the tube of the periscope has to be fifteen feet long. You see? It's easy."

Irene sighed. "It's marvelous," she said. "But don't you think it would be a lot easier if you just looked through these field glasses right into the window?"

Danny opened his mouth and closed it again. Joe began to laugh.

"Oh, well," Danny said ruefully. "I've heard that girls are more practical than boys."

Irene grinned, and handed him the binoculars. "You can have the first look, for saying such a nice thing," she said.

Danny peered at the laboratory window for a long moment, while the other two fidgeted. Then he said, "I can see a tall metal box. It has a square plate in it, something like a television screen."

"Let me look," Irene said.

"In a minute. I can see some other stuff—something that looks like a computer, with dials and buttons. Oh!"

"What? What is it?" Irene was almost dancing with impatience.

"The Professor!" Danny lowered the binoculars. "He was looking right at me. He shook his fist."

"What?" Irene snatched the field glasses. "That doesn't sound like him at all."

She lifted the binoculars to her eyes. Then

she snorted. "I see him all right, but he isn't shaking his fist, she said. "He's waving. Now he's bending over the table and doing something with a big piece of paper. Now he's at the outside door—he's opened it. He's holding up the paper. It's got writing on it."

"Writing? What does it say?"

"It says, 'I surrender. Come on in,' " she replied.

3
The Chronocycle

The three friends trooped rather sheepishly into the laboratory. It was a large room, ordinarily cluttered with a variety of equipment, but the Professor had pushed everything to one end to leave most of the space in the center empty. In the middle of the room stood a complex arrangement of machinery: a tall, narrow, steel cabinet with a frosted glass panel in its front, a network of oddly-shaped wires and metal rods, a thing that slightly resembled the programming panel of a computer with a series of flat buttons of different colors, and a number of other contraptions which the young people did not recognize and couldn't put a name to.

"I can take a hint," the Professor said,

with a chuckle. "I saw you all prowling about outside, creeping on the lawn and stalking, and then hurrying off to the woods. The sun reflected on something and I guessed that you were using a pair of binoculars. And at that point I realized that my behavior must have seemed very peculiar for the past few weeks and my friend Danny must have been going mad with curiosity."

He rested a gentle hand on Dan's shoulder. "Since I have always taught you that a scientist must be curious, my boy, I can't blame you. And now that I'm ready to test this equipment, I can take a moment to explain what I'm doing. Especially since I—"

He fell silent. Then, in an altered voice, he went on, "I won't beat around the bush. The test is going to be dangerous. This may be the last time we can talk together."

Danny felt a chill go through him at these words. His friends' faces were pale and startled. He said, "Professor! Do you mean that the—the test may—kill you?"

Irene clenched her hands together. "But that's terrible," she gasped. "Must you do it?"

Professor Bullfinch smiled again and took out his curved old pipe. He began to pack it carefully with tobacco. "Tut, tut! I'm surprised at you," he said. "A scientist has no time for fear. He must learn all he can, he must be constantly surprised and delighted at the marvelous things that lie waiting to be discovered. Death is only another experience. Those scientists who work with high voltages, with atomic radiation, with deadly poisons or the viruses of diseases, can't take the time to be afraid or nothing would ever be learned. Now that I've developed this temporal warp—" He gestured at the machine with a match and then lit his pipe. "Well, Dan, if you had found and developed a new principle, would you let someone else try it out for you?"

Danny shook his head. "Of course not. I—I think I understand."

"What does 'temporal warp' mean?" Irene asked, staring wide-eyed at the strange apparatus.

"Perhaps that's not such a good phrase for it. It means," said the Professor, "a twist in time."

"Saves nine?" said Joe.

They all laughed, and that relieved the tension. The Professor blew out a pale blue feather of smoke, and said, "Let me begin at the beginning. You know what time is, of course?"

"Well, sure we know," said Joe. "Seven-thirty, time for breakfast; twelve noon, time for lunch; six o'clock, time for dinner."

"And time for snacks in between," said Danny. "And snacks between snacks."

"I never eat between snacks," Joe said, with dignity.

"Then you think of time as something fixed to the clock?" said the Professor.

"No," Danny put in, "not just that. Because I remember your telling me that according to Einstein's Special Theory of Relativity time would be different for different observers."

"Just so," said the Professor. "It used to be thought that time was a kind of smoothly flowing river, in which *Now* was the same moment, or the same spot in that river, all through the universe. But our *Now* means only what's happening on this planet, Earth, spinning at a certain speed and revolving around our sun. If we could move out into space, *Now* would change. For instance, if a spaceship were to travel near the speed of light its time would be slower than time on earth. *Really* slower—a clock attached to something which is moving, runs more slowly than one which is standing still. A clock in a ship moving nearly as fast as light would run a great deal more slowly than a clock standing on a table and moving only as fast as our earth.

"We have to think of time as something different from the hours and minutes of our days, or the days of our years. Think of it as distance, for example. It might be the distance between one event and another, the distance between my lighting this pipe and then puffing out some smoke."

"If time is distance," Danny said, wrinkling up his nose in concentration, "then it's a way of measuring things."

"That's right. And it's a way of measuring which changes according to what's being measured. Let me give you an example."

There was a blackboard hanging on one wall of the laboratory. The Professor went to it and drew a diagram which looked like this:

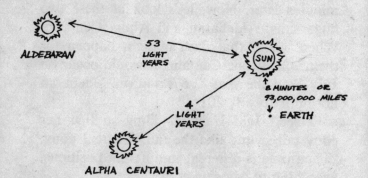

ALDEBARAN

53 LIGHT YEARS

SUN

8 MINUTES OR 93,000,000 MILES

• EARTH

4 LIGHT YEARS

ALPHA CENTAURI

"Let's say," he began, "that there are flame creatures living on our sun. At twelve o'clock noon, on July 1, 1963, they send out a brilliant flash of light, even brighter than sunlight. When would that flash of light 'happen'?"

"Wouldn't it happen at twelve noon?" Joe said, with surprise.

"No. Here on earth, it would 'happen' at 12:08 P.M. because it takes eight minutes for the light from our sun to reach us here on earth, jumping the 93 million miles between."

"Wait a minute!" Danny said. "That means we don't even really see our sun when we think we do."

"That's right," said Professor Bullfinch. "When we see the sun rise, we're actually seeing a ghost—the image of the sun eight minutes later. Now, let's look at these two huge suns, Aldebaran and Alpha Centauri. When would that flash of light happen for them? On Alpha Centauri it would occur on July 1, in the year 1967, and on Aldebaran not until July 1, 2016!"

"I see," said Irene, nodding so that her pony tail swung like the tail of a real pony. "Then time is different in different positions, according to where you are."

"Yes, that's it." The Professor put down the chalk and dusted his hands. He went to his strange machine and rested a hand on the upright metal case.

"Well, I began to think about moving in space and time," he went on. "I began to consider how it might be possible to move in time outside my position *here* and *now*. The result is this rather complicated—er—gadget."

He rubbed his bald head. "I've been trying to think of a name for it," he said. "For the time being, I call it the chronocycle—sort of a combination of chronometer, which is a timepiece, and—er—well—bicycle."

"A time machine!" Danny breathed.

"A time bicycle," Joe said, rather dazedly.

"Then you can go into the far distant future—a thousand years—and see all the wonderful inventions and—and everything?" said Irene.

"No, I'm afraid not. Not exactly," said the Professor. "What I think this apparatus will do is make limited computations forward in time and perhaps less limited predictions backward. It is very hard to explain to you, but in effect this machine will compute the possible position of atoms in space for some days or weeks in the future, or—since we know more about what has already happened —for a number of years in the past. It will then set up a probability curve, a kind of chart of the movement of objects in space and time. It will set up a field which warps, or twists, things inside that field out of the present moment and into a possible future or past."

He tapped the panel with the colored buttons. "This computing device—it's not really a computer, but I don't know what else to call it—with its own self-contained power pack, develops the graphs or diagrams of the possible future or possible past. The projections of the diagrams will appear on the screen of the control board." He pointed to the tall cabinet, and then to the tangle of wires and rods. "A relatively small spark is all I need to power the field. It is furnished by a condenser down there, which is fed by direct current from an outside source. The field is set up by these rods—I can't begin to explain how, at this moment. Perhaps later, after the test is over. Right now—" He emptied his pipe and tucked it into his pocket. "I'm going to have to chase you all out of here."

"Are you going to start the test now?" Danny had to gulp before he could get the words out.

"I am. And I don't want you youngsters in this laboratory when I start."

"But couldn't we just watch, from the corner of the room?" Danny said.

The Professor shook his head. "I don't mean to sound inhospitable," he answered, "but it's far too dangerous. I think I know what will happen, but I can't be sure. Something may go wrong. I may be whisked out of time altogether, or I may never be able to get back to this time. I don't want to take any chances with you three. I don't want you in this room."

Danny sighed. "Okay," he said, at last.

He turned to go. Then he swung back and impulsively threw his arms around the Professor and hugged him. "Gosh—be careful!" he said.

Irene kissed the Professor's cheek, and Joe shook hands with him gravely.

"It scares me," Irene said, "but it's so exciting, too. It's like one of those stories in which people can do magical things, like fly, or fight dragons, or make themselves invisible."

Professor Bullfinch took her gently by the shoulders and turned her to face the wall opposite the windows. Next to the blackboard there was a piece of paper with something lettered on it, set in a gold frame.

"Can you read that?" he said.

Irene read aloud:

The most beautiful and most profound emotion we can experience is the sensation of the mystical. It is the sower of all true science. He to whom this emotion is a stranger, who can no longer wonder and stand rapt in awe, is as good as dead.

—Albert Einstein

"Do you understand?" asked the Professor.

"Yes, I think so," said Irene.

The three went silently out of the room. The insant the laboratory door had closed, leaving them in the dark hallway, Danny grabbed Irene's wrist.

"I don't care what he says or how dangerous it is," he whispered fiercely. "I'm going to watch."

"Oh, Dan. Should you?" Irene said.

"Suppose something happens to him?" Danny replied. He was already in motion, dragging Irene behind him with Joe, looking gloomier than ever, bringing up the rear. "Suppose something goes wrong and he's hurt? And there'd be nobody here to help him. No, sir! I'm going to be right there—I got a first-aid merit badge in Scouting and even if I couldn't do anything for him I could still yell for help."

"But—but he said plainly that he didn't want us in that room with him," said Joe. "How can you just go back in there?"

"I'm not going back in there, and we won't be in the room with him," retorted Danny.

He led them through the dining room and the kitchen at a run, and out the kitchen door. He turned to the left. There was a window here, and this he very softly and carefully pushed up. He laid a finger on his lips and motioned the other two to follow him as he wriggled through the window like a red-headed serpent.

The Professor's laboratory actually consisted of two rooms: the larger, which was used for research, was the one in which the chronocycle now stood, but there was also a smaller one in which Professor Bullfinch kept his files, his notebooks, and his reference library. This was the room in which the three now stood. Danny tiptoed to the doorway and lay flat on the floor. Cautiously, he peeped around the edge of the door. Irene crouched next to him, her head only a little way above his. Joe clutched at his brow, blew out his lips soundlessly, and at last leaned above Irene and peered into the laboratory with the others.

They saw the Professor with his back to them, bending over the buttons of the computer. He straightened, and glanced around him at the various parts of his apparatus. He took a long, deep breath. He turned a dial and there was a faint humming sound. He threw a lever and at the same time touched a tiny switch set into the face of the upright metal case.

There was a *SNAP* which made them all jump. Then it seemed as if the sunlight were blotted out by a strange, murky grayness which settled over the laboratory and the study like a thick fog.

4
An Unexpected Visitor

To the three young people crouching in the Professor's study, it was as though night had suddenly fallen. Looking through the window behind him, Dan saw nothing but darkness. He turned back to the laboratory and found that he could no longer see the Professor, nor the chronocycle, nor even the far walls of the laboratory itself. Where the machine had been, there was a weird glow, vibrating and shimmering like the Northern Lights. In its midst he could make out the spiderweb of rods and coiled wires, shining with pale fire. The glow spread outward but oddly enough it did not seem to cast any light; rather, it appeared to penetrate all objects without making them appear more clearly. Even the details of the study—the desk and books and filing cabinets—vanished, and although Irene and Joe were right beside him he had difficulty making out their forms.

The hair rose on the back of his neck. He found that he was chewing on his lower lip until it hurt. He heard Irene gasp, and then another sound, a faint clicking, which he couldn't identify until suddenly he realized that it was the chattering of Joe's teeth.

Then, as abruptly as it had come, the darkness lifted. All three let out their breath in long sighs.

The Professor still stood before the chronocycle. Nothing had changed.

Before he could stop himself, Danny blurted, "It didn't work!"

The Professor's head snapped up and he stared about. Then he said, "Dan! Where are you?"

Slowly Danny got to his feet and walked out into the laboratory, his face almost as red as his hair.

Professor Bullfinch blinked at him, took off his glasses with a helpless air, put them on again, and said, "Danny, what am I to do with you? After I told you I didn't want you in the lab during the experiment—"

"I know, Professor. But I was afraid something might happen to you. I could see you just lying here on the floor, maybe badly hurt or—or electrocuted—or something, and I *had* to be around where I could help you."

The Professor's round face lighted with a smile. "Oh, good heavens, Dan," he said. "How can I scold you?"

"Anyway, we weren't in the lab," Danny went on.

"We? Oh, yes, I might have known. The others are with you, I suppose."

Joe and Irene came out into view.

"Well, there's no point in telling you how foolish you all were," said Professor Bullfinch. "You've always been headstrong, Dan, and in this case maybe there was some justification for what you did."

Danny grinned with relief. "Anyhow, the chronocycle didn't work, did it?" he said. "So we didn't have to worry after all."

The Professor took his chin in his hand. "That's just it," he said. "I'm not sure whether it worked or not. *Something* happened. There was a sort of dark fog all around me—"

"Oh, we saw it. It was all around us, too," said Irene.

"Hmm. It was? Then obviously the field stretches further than I thought," mused the Professor. "Whatever happened, you were affected by it as well as I. I think that mist was the timewarp field. Perhaps what happened was that we were sent forward in time while the fog was around us, and then returned when I shut off the machine."

Joe craned his neck to look at the glass screen. "Doesn't this thing have some kind of mileage record, Professor Bullfinch? I mean, I always thought a time machine would have a dial marked off with years—50 B.C., or 2000 A.D.—so you'd know how far you traveled."

The Professor chuckled. "I'm afraid my chronocycle is a crude model, Joe," he said. "It doesn't even have a speedometer."

Danny was examining the switches on the front of the cabinet. "Well, how do you make it go forward or backward?" he asked.

Professor Bullfinch indicated a bank of instruments on the front of the cabinet. "This dial," he explained, "sets the strength of the field. This is the master control lever which sets off the spark activating the field. This switch starts the computer calculating forward or backward from the present instant."

He tapped the glass screen. "The field pulsates," he went on, "and its pulses are shown on this screen."

He stopped, his finger still outstretched. "Ah, very interesting," he said.

"What's the matter?" Danny asked. "Something wrong?"

"Oh, no. But look here."

The three followed his pointing finger. On the glass screen was a short black line with three small peaks, like tiny mountains, rising from it.

"This seems to show that we did actually move in time," the Professor said. "I set the field at a very, very low strength and the computing lever for *forward*. In the dark, the screen glowed but I didn't notice this mark. Apparently, after the machine is shut off the mark remains."

"And the mark shows that we did move forward?" said Irene.

"Mhm." The Professor was busy with a ruler. "The peaks are one-quarter of an inch apart," he said. He turned to the computer panel. "I'm going to start the computer calculating backward in time, now, without activating the field," he said. "Let's see if a line will appear on the screen."

He pushed the switch. At once, the line

with its jagged peaks began moving very rapidly from left to right across the screen.

"Most interesting indeed," said the Professor. "You see, I didn't anticipate that the pulses would show up as a line independently of the motion of the chronocycle. Now, let me see, next time I conduct a test I should perhaps measure the length of the line. Then I may be able to determine how far I have gone."

He glanced sharply at the three youngsters over the rims of his glasses. "But next time," he said, "you won't be around. No hiding anywhere! You'll be at a safe distance, and I'll let you know afterward what the result was."

"But Professor!" Danny yelped. "Now you know there's no danger. Why can't we go with you?"

"Hey, wait a minute," said Joe. "What's this 'we' stuff? You can go. I'm not going on any bicycling trip into the age of disosaurs."

Irene had been watching the screen. "The black line is still going, Professor," she said.

"Ah, yes. Time I shut that off." Professor Bullfinch put out a hand for the switch.

At that instant, the outer door of the laboratory opened and Joe stepped in.

"Hi," he said, closing the door behind him. "What are you all doing in here?"

"Hi, what are you all doing in here?"

"What are we doing?" Danny's voice died away, although his mouth went right on opening and shutting.

Irene said, "Joe! Where—" She swallowed hard. "Where did you come from?"

The Professor was staring in amazement from the Joe who had just come in to the Joe who stood beside the chronocycle. For once, he had lost his calm appearance.

"What do you mean, where did I—?" The new Joe suddenly caught sight of the other Joe. "Eeek!" he screeched.

The Joe who was standing at the chronocycle control panel, was as white and quivering as a bowl of custard. "I—I—you—" he stammered.

Suddenly, he uttered a shriek of terror. "Let's get out of here!" he yelled. "We're in the future! We're in the future! There are too many of me!"

He grabbed for the controls. Danny leaped at him.

"Not that one," Danny shouted.

They struggled for a moment, and fell sideways. Danny's elbow hit a lever. There was a loud snap. And once again, everything grew dim and foggy as the time field extended its shimmering halo around them.

5
Possible Joe

For a few minutes there was terrible confusion in the gloom, as people stumbled about and bumped into each other and groaned and whimpered and squealed with pain as they hit each other or various hard surfaces.

The Professor called, "Stand still, everyone! You might damage the machinery."

By degrees, everything grew quiet.

"I'll shut off the chronocycle," the Professor muttered. "Where is it? Who's standing near it? Danny?"

"I—I'm not sure, Professor," Danny said, in a muffled voice. "In the first place, I'm not standing. I'm on the floor. There's something next to me. Wait a minute." After a bit, he said, "It's metal, all right, but I don't think it's the control board. It's too low."

"All right, don't touch anything," said the Professor. "Heaven knows what that is. Just a moment. I'll try to find the dratted thing."

They could just make out his dim shape moving through the pale glow. "Ouch!" he said. "Drat! That's not it."

"Professor," Irene said. "The time field is fading."

The unearthly Northern Lights of the time field were indeed flickering out. The glow vanished, and they were in darkness. They waited for the sunlight to reappear as it had the first time, but after a long couple of minutes all was still black. Not quite solid black, however, for as their eyes grew accustomed to it they all saw a number of paler oblongs at intervals around them.

"It's night," Danny exclaimed. "That's why it's dark. It's nighttime and those are the windows of the lab, and the glass of the outer door. Look—you can see the stars."

"Then we have certainly moved in time," said the Professor.

He lit a match and blinked anxiously over the tiny flame. Cupping his hand around it, he groped toward the wall. They heard the sharp clicking as he tried the light switch.

"All the fuses must have blown out," he said. "No lights."

"Isn't there a big flashlight hanging near the outside door, Professor?" Danny said.

The match suddenly went out and the Professor said, "Ow! Wait a minute while I light another match."

Once again, the tiny flower of flame blossomed in his fingers. He fumbled along the wall and soon found the flashlight. He snapped it on and threw its bright beam around the room.

"Whew!" he said. "Everybody here? Nobody hurt?"

"I'm here," said Danny.

"I'm all right," Irene said.

"I'm here," said Joe.

"Oh, no!" wailed Joe. "Did you hear that? I didn't say that. It was *him*—the other one."

The flashlight beam picked out his face. He was standing beside Danny, on one side of the computer. The beam wavered away from him and traveled around the room again until it came to rest on a second Joe. This one, looking as scared as the first, was standing on the far side of the control board.

"What—what does he mean 'the other one'?" said this second Joe. "I'm me. Who's he?"

"Now, let's all try to keep calm," said the Professor, in a shaking voice. "Let's try to think this through."

He flashed the light from one Joe to the other. Then he said, "Joe."

"Yes," said two voices at once.

"No, I mean the Joe who was already in the laboratory, not the one who came in later."

"That's me," said the Joe who was standing next to Danny.

"Ah. Let's see how you're dressed." The light flicked from his head to his feet. "Blue dungarees, a red and white striped shirt— slightly dirty—a blue denim jacket, sneakers. Good. Now let's look at the other one. Blue dungarees—oh, dear. I'm afraid that's no good. They're both dressed exactly alike."

"It's what I always wear—except on Sundays and special days," said the second Joe, mournfully.

"How does he know that?" said the first Joe, clutching at Danny's arm.

Professor Bullfinch snapped his fingers. "Aha!" he said. "I have it. Joe One—the Joe who was here with us. What day is it?"

"Why, it's—gosh! I don't remember. Oh, yes, it's Saturday."

"And what date?"

"It's—it's—the twenty-seventh of April."

"He's crazy," said the second Joe. "It's Tuesday, the twenty-ninth of April. That proves it. He's an imposter."

There was a long silence, broken by Irene saying, "But it *is* Saturday. It was this morning when we got together to study."

The Professor said, slowly, "I see. Great heavens! We moved forward that first time I operated the chronocycle. We moved forward three days, from Saturday to Tuesday. We moved into a *possible* future Tuesday. The first Joe is the Joe who went with us, of course. And this other Joe—"

"What about him?" gasped Irene.

"This other Joe is a *possible* Joe."

"Wh—wh—what do you mean 'possible'?" stuttered the second Joe. "Do you mean I'm—I'm not real?"

"I don't know," said the Professor, in a baffled tone. "I'm afraid I haven't enough information to be able to say anything definite. The computer, using all the facts at its disposal, calculates a possible future time. In that possible future, it was possible for Joe to walk into the laboratory. When we returned to our present time, we brought him back with us. If that future Tuesday turns out to be an actual future day, then he is real."

"Oooh, golly," said the second Joe. He slumped back against the metal case of the chronocycle. "This is awful. I feel like me. I feel real. How can we find out whether I *am* real?"

Professor Bullfinch rubbed his bald head. "We might simply live through the next three days," he said. "If that Tuesday is the Tuesday you came from, then the two Joes will simply merge together into one."

"And if not, I'll vanish!" said the second Joe. "Is that it? Oh, no. I don't want to vanish! Help, help!"

Danny grabbed him by both arms. "Stop it, Joe," he said. "It won't do any good to yell. Anyway, it isn't that bad. We can just set the chronocycle three days ahead and ship you back to your own possible future."

The second Joe wiped his forehead. "Yes, I guess that's so. Isn't it, Professor?"

Professor Bullfinch nodded, looking pleased. "It is certainly a possibility," he said.

"Oh, don't use that word," groaned the first Joe.

The second Joe was looking a good deal more cheerful. "Okay," he said, "what's the use of hollering? I've got an idea."

"I know just what he's going to say," said the first Joe. "Let's go into the kitchen and see if there's anything to eat."

"Gee, maybe we are both me," said the second Joe. "We think the same way. We may as well be friends."

He held out his hand. The first Joe took it.

"I don't mind telling you, this is a very unusual feeling," he said, as they shook hands.

Danny shook hands with the other Joe, too. "Greetings, Possible," he said. "I guess that's what we'd better call you. We can't call you both Joe."

"Well, there's no point in standing here in the dark," said the Professor. "Let's go fix that fuse and see what time it really is. And you kids can find a little snack in the refrigerator while I'm doing that."

He strode to the inner door and pulled it open. "Ulp!" he said.

The children crowded around to stare at what the flashlight showed. Instead of the hallway leading from the laboratory, there was a solid, blank wooden wall on the other side of the door.

6
Father Abraham's Almanack

Professor Bullfinch put out a trembling hand and touched the wall. "Bless my soul!" he said.

"Where did that come from?" Danny asked in a hushed voice.

The Professor turned away. "Follow me," he said. "Let's get outside and take a look at things."

He led the way to the outside door. The night was mild and pleasant and full of the scents of spring. He turned the flashlight toward the house.

"Anyway, it's still there," said Irene. "Did you think it had vanished?"

"Frankly, I don't know what I thought," the Professor said.

They followed him around the corner of the house to the front door. All was dark and quiet, not only in the house but all about them, as if all of Midston were asleep. The Professor swept the light back and forth over the front of the house. "It's my house all right," he murmured. He tried the door. It appeared to be locked.

He knocked loudly. "Mrs. Dunn!" he called. "Let's us in."

"It's spooky," said Possible.

"It reminds me of a movie I once saw," Joe said, shakily. "I was called *The Monster from the Hidden Depths.*"

"Ooh, yeah," said Possible. "These people came to an old house on a hilltop at midnight, and they knocked at the door, and it creaked slowly open and there was this Thing—"

"It's opening!" Irene squealed. She grabbed Danny's hand.

Involuntarily, they all fell back a step as the door swung wide.

"Er—I'm sorry, Mrs. Dunn," the Professor began.

But it wasn't Mrs. Dunn. A thin, elderly man stood before them holding a candlestick aloft. He wore a heavy, dark-red dressing gown and on his head was a white stocking cap with a tassel which fell to his shoulder.

"I beg your pardon," said the Professor.

"How can I help you, sir?" said the elderly man.

"Why I—is—is this the house of Professor Euclid Bullfinch?" asked the Professor.

"Alas, no," said the man. "The house is mine. There is no Professor here, neither Bullfinch nor other."

"I see." The Professor cleared his throat. "Well, is this the town of Midston?"

"Yes, this is Middestown. But I know of no Professor Bullfinch here."

He glanced past the Professor at the four huddled young people.

"However, I fear the late hour has sent my courtesy to the winds, sir," he continued. "It is clear to me that you are lost, and here I keep you and your children standing on the doorstone. Please come in, the night air is chill and you must be a-weary."

The Professor hesitated. Then he said, "You're very kind, sir. Come on, kids."

They entered the house, and Danny stared about in astonishment. It was the same house and yet there were differences which leaped out at him even by the uncertain candlelight. The hall seemed smaller, somehow, until he realized that the familiar wallpaper with its bright design of wreaths was gone. Instead the walls were painted a rather drab tan. The stairway was plain, dark wood instead of being white. The stranger led them into the parlor to the left, and here, although the fireplace with its heavy beam and overmantle, and the small-paned windows, and the wide floor boards were all as he remembered them, the furnishing had mysteriously changed. Gone were the comfortable overstuffed armchairs, the couch, the bookshelves, and the television set. Instead, there were three or four straight chairs, a heavy pine table, and two rather stiff-looking wooden armchairs. A few books in thick leather bindings lay on the table, and there were candles in tin sconces fastened to the walls. Here, too, the wallpaper had vanished; there was plain wooden paneling on the fireplace wall, and the other walls were smooth plaster. There was no rug on the floor, and the room seemed rather chilly and bare.

Their host set his candlestick on the table. He took up a long taper, lighted it at the candle, and touched it to several of the other candles on the walls. Then he turned to face them, with his hands clasped behind his back.

Danny said, in a very small voice, "Couldn't we t-t-telephone somebody and find out where we are?"

Their host said, "Alack, child, I fear I do not understand you. You are in Middestown as you desired. But we have here no tetetephelone, whatever that may be."

Irene drew closer to Danny. "I'm scared," she whispered.

Another voice said, "What's amiss, Jonathan?"

They turned to see a second man in the doorway. He carried a candle in a flat saucer-shaped holder. He wore a flowered dressing gown and his head was wrapped in a cloth, something like a very sloppy turban. He was stout and jovial-looking, with a round face, a short upturned nose, and a firm, square jaw.

"Why, Ben, some strays, I fear," said their host. "Foreigners, I think likely, by their talk."

"We are *not* foreigners," Danny said. "We're Americans."

"Indeed?" said the man called Ben. "We'll not deny you that, my boy, and no doubt as good subjects of His Majesty as we, yet your clothes are certainly of a cut strange to me. But 'pon my soul, Jon, why do we keep these good folk standing about? They must be bone-weary if they are lost, as you say, and hungry too, I'll be bound."

"Oh, man, you can say that again," said Joe, gratefully.

"Why should I say it again?" said Ben. "Ah, I see, that was merely an expression of pleasure, eh?"

"Yes, yes, pray sit down—all of you," said Jonathan. "I'll fetch a collation. Ben, do you settle 'em, please."

The Professor sank into one of the armchairs. "Phew!" he said. "Suddenly, I feel exhausted."

"Me, too," said Danny. "I feel as if we've been on our feet for days."

"Maybe we have," Joe said, in a strained voice. "Who knows *how* long we've been going?"

The man named Ben surveyed them with a beaming smile. "All your children, sir?" he said to the Professor. "My congratulations."

"Oh, no, no. Not mine," said the Professor. Then he shrugged. "That is—well, I suppose I am responsible for them."

"And have you traveled far?"

The five exchanged glances. "Well," the Professor began, "that's difficult to say. I want to ask you—"

But at that moment, Jonathan returned. He was laden with a pitcher, five pewter mugs, and a basket in which was a loaf of coarse gray bread, a lump of yellow cheese, and a knife. He set the things on the table and poured milk into the cups, while Ben cut up the bread and cheese and passed it around.

"Pray, refresh yourselves," said Jonathan. "I am sorry that I cannot furnish you with better fare, but the hour is late and my housekeeper sleeps like the dead and will not rouse for anything until cock-crow."

The young people fell on the food ravenously. Professor Bullfinch sipped a little milk, and then said, "Gentlemen, I thank you for your hospitality. But I must ask you something which I fear is going to sound very odd. May I beg you to bear with me, and answer me, no matter how queer my question seems?"

Ben pursed up his lips. "Sir," he replied, "I daresay I have, in the course of my life, heard many questions which sounded as though the askers had taken leave of their wits. But I pride myself on being a philosopher, and I know that a singular question sometimes conceals an interesting idea. Ask what you will."

"Very well, then." The Professor sat up straight. "What year is this?"

"What year?" said Jonathan, in surprise.

Ben, without a word, went to the table. He took up a small book, opened it to the title page, and handed it to the Professor. Professor Bullfinch blinked at it through his glasses. He held it a little closer to the candle flame. Then he read, aloud:

"Father Abraham's Almanack, for the Year of Our Lord, 1763."

7
Captives of the Clevelands

The four children sat in stunned silence, as Professor Bullfinch very deliberately closed the almanac and placed it on the table.

At last, Danny said, "Wow! 1763!"

The Professor shot him a quick glance. "That'll do, Dan," he said, warningly. "And the rest of you—keep cool. Let's not lose our heads. Let me handle this."

Danny suddenly understood. He sat back and said to the others, in a low voice, "He's right. Let's just keep quiet."

Professor Bullfinch turned to the two men. "Gentlemen," he said, "I suppose I owe you an explanation. The truth is, I hardly know where to begin. Perhaps I'd better introduce myself. I am—er—ah—George Smith. I'm a—well—a sort of schoolmaster."

Both men bowed politely.

"My name, sir, is Jonathan Turner," said the thinner one. "And this is my friend Mr. Franklin, Benjamin Franklin, of Philadelphia."

Five pairs of eyes swiveled toward the stout man, and five mouths dropped open.

Irene said, "Benjamin Franklin! Oh, my goodness! The real, true Benjamin Franklin?"

Mr. Franklin laughed. "There, Jonathan, what greater reason for pride could a man have than such wholehearted commendation from the young? My dear child, I hope I am the real Ben Franklin, and I shall do my best to be true."

The Professor jumped to his feet. "This is a very great honor, Mr. Franklin," he said. "Allow me to shake hands with you."

"Me, too," cried Danny.

The two Joes and Irene crowded behind him, and for a moment the room seemed much too small for all that handshaking. Then the Professor motioned the young people to their chairs again, and himself sat down. Mr. Franklin was red-cheeked with pleasure.

He said, "I thank you all. Had His Majesty sent me a marshal's staff, I think I could scarce have been so proud of it as I am of your esteem."

Mr. Turner nodded. "It is most gratifying," he said. "Now, sir, let us hear the rest of your story."

"Ah, yes," said Professor Bullfinch. "Where was I? Um . . . you see, these four youngsters and I were studying natural history. We were investigating the life history of the butterfly. Our researches took us into the field where we were looking for cocoons, and suddenly we were—uh—we were captured by Indians."

Joe said, "We were?" Then, catching himself, he said, "I mean, yes. We were!"

"They carried us with them over the mountains," the Professor continued. "And we were held prisoner by them for a long time. A very long time. At last, we escaped."

"Amazing!" Mr. Turner said. "How did you manage it?"

"How? Well, we . . . er—how? Ah, we disguised ourselves," the Professor said, rather desperately. "And in disguise we crept out of the Indian camp one night, stole five horses, and rode away. We traveled for many miles, and at last found ourselves near this village. I must have mistaken the name of the village and thought it was another place where I have a friend, Professor Bullfinch, who could help us return to our home. Now you see why we didn't even know what year it was."

"An astonishing tale," said Mr. Franklin. "And your clothes—those odd garments you are wearing?"

"These were our disguise," said the Professor, triumphantly.

"I see." Mr. Franklin shook his head. "I am deeply grieved at this account of trouble with the Indians. And were your captors members of the Six Nations, Mr. Smith?"

"The Six Nations? Oh, no. I don't think so. They were—" The Professor looked uneasily about him. He could not, for the life of him, think of the name of a single Indian tribe.

Joe broke in, "They were Cleveland Indians."

"Clevelands?" Mr. Turner raised his eyebrows. "I don't think I have ever heard of such a tribe."

"Well, you see, they must have come from the far West," said the Professor quickly.

"Yes, they weren't dressed like other Indians."

"Well, sir, happily your ordeal is over," said Mr. Turner. "You shall spend the night with me here, and in the morning we will see what we can do to return you to your home. Where is your home, by the by?"

"In Midston," the Professor said, without thinking. "Oh, I'm sorry. I guess I'm beginning to feel tired. We live in—in—in Chicago."

"Chicago? I don't think I know it. In what province is it?"

"It's just a little village, a tiny village," the Professor said, wearily. "You'd never have heard of it. It's in Maine."

Mr. Turner picked up his candlestick. "We'll speak no more tonight," he said. "I can see how fatigued you are. Now, Ben, where shall we bed down these good folk?"

"I can give up my room to Mr. Smith," Mr. Franklin was beginning.

The Professor said, "No, no. I can't allow any fuss to be made. In the first place, after our terrible experiences, I think these youngsters would be happier if they weren't separated from each other or from me. Isn't that right, kids?"

"Sure," said Danny. "Why not just give us

some blankets and let us sleep right here, on
the floor? I wouldn't mind that. Would you,
Irene?"

"Oh, no," said Irene. "It would be fun. It
would be like camping out."

"What's so much fun about camping out?"
grumbled Possible, but Danny nudged him
in the ribs, and he subsided.

"It's a mild night," the Professor continued, "and we will be perfectly comfortable."

It seemed Mr. Turner was about to dis-
agree, when Mr. Franklin put in, "If that is
what they wish, Jonathan, why not give in?
Surely, Mr. Smith knows best what he and
his children want."

"Very well, Ben," said Mr. Turner, "although it shames me to have 'em sleep on
the floor."

He bustled off and Mr. Franklin went
along to help him. They returned with their
arms full of blankets. The boys had moved
back the furniture, and as they began spread-
ing out the blankets, Mr. Turner handed the
Professor a tasseled cap like the one he himself wore.

"I see that you wear your own hair, sir,"
he said, "yet perhaps you will be grateful for
this."

"Eh? Oh—yes, thanks very much," said the Professor.

"I trust you will sleep well. Good night to you."

"Good night," said Professor Bullfinch, pulling the nightcap down over his ears.

However, the instant the footsteps of the two men had died away on the stair, the Professor whipped off the cap and whispered, "Don't go to sleep, any of you!"

"How can we sleep?" Irene said, sitting up. "I'm too excited ever to go to sleep again."

"You bet!" Danny breathed. "Benjamin Franklin! Just think of it! And Mr. Turner —the man our house was built for."

"What did he mean when he said that you wear your own hair, Professor?" Irene asked.

"Why, most of the men in this age wear wigs, my dear," said the Professor. "It's the fashion. That's one reason they wear nightcaps—their heads are shaved, or their hair cut very short, and the night caps keep them snug."

Joe wrapped his arms around his knees. "Now, listen," he said. "I went along with that gag about being captured by Indians because I thought Professor Bullfinch must have had a good reason for it. But I don't get it."

"That's right," said Possible. "What was all that stuff about you being George Smith, Professor? I nearly burst, trying to keep from laughing."

"Oh, you idiots," said Danny. "What would *you* have told them?"

"Why, I'd have just said that we—I mean, I'd have told them that—hmm, I see what you mean," said Joe.

Possible slowly nodded. "I see, too. They'd have thought we were ready to be carried away in straitjackets if we had told them we came from two hundred years in the future."

"Yes, and since the Professor had already asked if this was the house of Professor Bullfinch, he couldn't then say he was Professor Bullfinch," Irene said.

"That's right," said the Professor. "Now, our only chance is to wait until they're asleep again and then slip out to the chronocycle and get back to our own time as quickly as we can."

He chuckled softly. "I must say, I hate to do it. I'd certainly like to have a chance to talk to Mr. Franklin for an hour or two. But it's much too risky. Lie down, now, and be as patient as you can. Don't even talk—they might hear you and become suspicious."

Danny lay back with his head pillowed on

his arms, staring at the beams in the ceiling. The same beams! he thought. There they were, but new-looking, with rough plaster between them. In his own time they were darker, and between them the plaster was smooth and white. "I'll never be able to sit in this room again without thinking of being here two hundred years ago," he said to himself. He glanced at the fireplace and could just make out the initials "J.T." burned into the heavy chimney beam. "Jonathan Turner," he thought. "I've actually seen and talked to the man who put those initials there. I wonder what the rest of the house looks like . . . ?"

He suddenly felt the Professor shaking him by the shoulder, and realized that he had dozed off in the middle of the thought. He scrambled up, almost falling flat on his nose as his legs tangled in the blankets. Irene was already up and carefully folding her blankets by the light of a single candle on the wall. Joe and Possible struggled to their feet yawning, and in a few minutes they were all ready.

The Professor took his flashlight out of his pocket and pinched out the wick of the candle. "I wish we could leave our friends a note," he said, "but I'd rather not take the time. Come on. And for heaven's sake, be as quiet as mice."

The front door, they found, had no lock. Instead, it was held shut by an iron bolt. Professor Bullfinch had taken the candle with him, and he rubbed it carefully on the bolt and the hinges of the door. "I hope this works," he muttered. "I saw it done in a movie when I was fifteen years old." Very slowly, inch by inch, he drew back the bolt. Just as slowly, he pulled the door open. It gave a slight squeak.

"It's just us mice," whispered Possible.

The Professor slipped outside. He turned off the flashlight, for the starry night was bright enough for them to find their way. They slipped around the corner of the house and crept to what had once been—or would someday be, depending on how you thought about it—their back yard. There was the Professor's laboratory looming up darkly against the rear of the house. The outline of the house itself had not changed in two hundred years, and everything looked so normal that Danny could hardly believe they had really made the trip back into time.

Professor Bullfinch opened the outer door of the laboratory and they all hurried inside.

He snapped on the flashlight again, and counted noses.

"All here? Nobody left behind?"

"We're all here and ready," said Possible. "Let's get started for home."

"Gee, that sounds funny," said Joe. "Danny and the Professor *are* home, and yet they aren't."

"Gather round the machine," the Professor said. "I don't want to take the slightest chance."

He reached for the master lever.

The outer door flew open with a bang!

"Aha! Extremely interesting," said a familiar voice.

There stood Mr. Franklin, holding two flintlock pistols which to the startled visitors from the twentieth century appeared to be as large as cannons. Behind him, and looking rather flurried and nervous, was Mr. Turner holding up a lantern.

"And now," said Mr. Franklin, in a voice that was cool, precise, and not at all jolly, "perhaps Mr. Smith, or whatever you call yourself, you'll explain to us what this is all about."

8
Stranded in the Past

Much later, Danny was to remember the utter strangeness of that scene: the deep shadows out of which peered staring faces lighted by the yellow lantern and the bright beam of the flashlight, the contrast between the shining machinery of the chronocycle and the ancient pistols which Mr. Franklin held steadily pointed at them. But now, his only sensation was of horrified shock.

"Tell him, Professor!" he cried. "Don't let him shoot! We're from the future!"

"From the—" Mr. Franklin said. The pistols wavered in his hands. He tried again, "From the—" He looked all around the laboratory as if seeing it for the first time. Then, in a rather faint voice, he said, "I think perhaps I'd better sit down."

Mr. Turner said, "I don't believe it. It isn't possible."

"Ooh, there's that word again," said Joe. "Tell him, Professor Bullfinch. *Anything* is possible!"

"I'm afraid so," said the Professor. "Danny! Joe! There's a bench at the far end of the room, among that equipment. Lug it out, please."

The boys ran and got the bench. They put it near the chronocycle, and the two men sank gratefully down on it. Mr. Turner put his lantern on the floor and regarded the computer and the control board with its levers and glass screen.

"Ben," he said, in a hushed tone, "there's nothing like this in our world. And by what magic could they erect a whole building—?"

Mr. Franklin drew a deep breath. "Mr. Smith—is that your real name, by the way?" he said.

"No. I am Professor Euclid Bullfinch."

"I see. I presume we will hear everything in due course. But I must tell you this: Mr. Turner and I are Natural Philosophers. We have, in our own ways, attempted to study the laws of Nature and to inquire sincerely into the truth. I think, sir, that we are better able than most men to deal fairly and coolly with whatever you may have to tell us. We shall listen to you without fear and with open minds."

"That's what I hope I would have said myself, if I were in your shoes," said the Professor. "Very well, gentlemen. The fact is, we have come from a time two hundred years in your future by means of this invention, the chronocycle. I don't see how I can explain how it works, since our science is so vastly different from yours and so much has happened in the two hundred years between us —I simply can't put the matter into words you would understand. Our coming here was something of an accident, and in fact we didn't even know we were in the past until I tried to get into my house. I beg your pardon, Mr. Turner—*your* house, but in my own time, it's mine."

"I see," Mr. Turner said. "Then two hundred years from now, my house is still standing and is lived in by a learned man?" He shook his head. "I must say, it gives me a great deal of pleasure to know that."

"I'm sorry we had to put you to so much trouble," said the Professor. "And I'm sorry, too, that I had to tell you all those fibs about being captured by Indians. But you will understand the reason."

"I think we do," said Mr. Franklin. "I was suspicious of you, you know. Your clothing, your speech—and your hair was very short for a man who had lived among Indians so long a time. When Jonathan and I went to get the blankets, I said to him, 'Let them sleep where they will, and we will lie in wait. If the rascals try any tricks we'll catch 'em red-handed.' We heard you leave the house and pursued you, but all my suspicions could not have anticipated *this*."

"Now, gentlemen, we want to return to our own time as quickly as possible," said the Professor. "I hope you will keep our secret—"

"Keep it? We're in the same boat as you, my dear sir," cried Mr. Franklin. "Who would believe us if we told 'em we were visited by a man from the future?" He sighed, wistfully. "Wonders untold," he said. "What wonders you must have, in your day! I've half a mind to go back with you. Eh, Jonathan? What do you say?"

Mr. Turner snorted. "Not for me, Ben. I like my comfortable life, my snug house, and my studies. I should find the future very unsettling, I fear. And so should you."

"Quite true," said Mr. Franklin. "And yet —I have so many questions."

"There's a great deal I can never tell you, Mr. Franklin," said the Professor gravely. "It isn't a blessing for a man to know his future. Don't you agree?"

"I do, sir."

"But there are some things I can say. For one thing, these Colonies of yours, by our day, have become the greatest country in the world. Men have conquered many diseases, they have learned how to fly, how to leave the earth's surface and go into outer space, how to descend to the depths of the ocean. We are probing the nature of the atom and the structure of the universe itself."

Mr. Franklin watched him in fascination. "Amazing!" he said. "And yet, not so amazing after all. One might guess at it. How much there is to be learned! As long as there are inquiring minds, there will be no secrets. And these young people—they are your students?"

"This boy, Danny, is almost a son to me," said the Professor. "The others are his friends —and mine."

Mr. Franklin got to his feet. "I have much to think about," he said. "We will not detain you longer. May we watch you depart?"

"I'm afraid not," said the Professor. "At least, not from inside the laboratory. The time field seems to cover this entire structure, and you'd be whisked forward with us. You can watch from outside, though. And Mr. Franklin—"

"Yes?"

"There's one more thing I'd like to say to you. Remember that when we first heard your name, we all knew who you were although we came from the distant future."

Mr. Franklin drew himself up. "I do remember," he said. "No one could ask for more. Come, Jonathan."

They bowed deeply to Professor Bullfinch, and left the lab.

Danny said, in a hushed voice, "Now you can say that Benjamin Franklin visited your laboratory. Only nobody will believe you."

The Professor clapped his hands. "We'll discuss it all when we're safely back in our own time," he said. "Get set. Here we go."

He threw the master lever and touched the switch.

Nothing happened.

"What on earth—?" he mumbled.

Once again, he snapped the switch. There was no answering hum or crackle from the machine, no gathering fog.

"Something's wrong," said Danny.

The Professor took off his glasses and rubbed his eyes with the heel of his hand. "I give up," he said. "It's much too dark to investigate now. We'll have to take advantage of Mr. Turner's offer, and stay the night."

"But—but—" Joe said. "You mean we're stuck here in the eighteenth century? We can't get back again?"

"What'll happen? Everybody will start wondering where we are," cried Possible. "And even the laboratory will be missing. They'll think it was stolen!"

"Now, now, calm down," said Professor Bullfinch, picking up the flashlight. "Things aren't quite that bad. First of all, I'm sure I'll be able to fix the chronocycle as soon as it's light enough for me to see what I'm doing. I can't manage all the connections with nothing more than this flashlight, which is beginning to wear out anyway. And I do feel somehow very tired, so that I wouldn't trust myself with delicate wiring. Anyway, when we return, we'll return to a time a few minutes after we left. So we won't have been gone for more than that few minutes, as far as anyone at home is concerned. Understand?"

Joe's eyes were round with wonder. "I—I

guess so," he said. "You mean we'll get back right after we left."

"Suppose we get back *before* we left?" said Possible.

"Let's not worry about that now," said Professor Bullfinch. He pulled open the door and called into the darkness, "Mr. Turner! I think I'll want that nightcap, after all."

9
Breakfast and
a Discovery

Danny opened his eyes and lay for a moment, looking at the ceiling and trying to remember his queer dream. He had dreamed he had gone into the past and had met Benjamin Franklin! It must have started with all that talk about history, and the Professor telling him about Jonathan Turner's initials in the chimney beam.

Initials! Chimney beam! Mr. Turner! He sat upright. It was no dream after all: he was rolled in a blanket on the parlor floor of Mr. Turner's house and the first rays of the sun were gilding the small, thick panes of the windows.

Danny struggled to his feet and stared outside. "It's true," he whispered. "And golly—it's all changed."

A dusty road ran before the house, rutted by the tracks of wagons. The paved streets he knew were gone, as were the telephone poles, the automobiles, and most of the familiar houses. One of the houses across the way had a thatched roof like one he had seen in a picture of an English village, and there was a cow grazing in front of it behind a wooden rail fence. Opposite, there was a long-barreled musket came out of the cabin, glanced up at the sky, spat lazily into the dust, and went trudging off. He was wearing a coonskin cap and a fringed leather jacket.

"Did you see that? Did you see how he was dressed?" Irene joined Danny at the window, along with Joe and Possible.

"Maybe it was Kit Carson," said Joe.

"Maybe you'd better study your history," Danny grinned. "Kit Carson isn't going to be born for another forty years or more."

"Isn't it wonderful?" said Irene. "Isn't it exciting?"

"It'll be even more exciting when we find out one thing," said Possible, combing his hair out of his eyes with his fingers.

"You mean, whether the Professor can fix the chronocycle?" said Dan.

"Nope. I mean what's for breakfast," Possible replied.

"A boy after my own heart," said Joe enthusiastically, putting his arm around his twin's shoulders. "Shall we go, partner?"

"Your servant, sir," Possible said, bowing in imitation of Mr. Turner.

The Professor was sitting up, rubbing his eyes. "Good morning," he said. "You know, sleeping with a nightcap on isn't such a bad notion. Keeps your brain nice and warm. I must try it when we get home. How are you all?"

"Fine, Professor," Danny said. "We're just going to see how much the kitchen has changed."

"Ow!" The Professor winced as he began to rise. "I guess I'm out of practice sleeping on floors. Go ahead, and I'll join you as soon as I can get the stiffness out of my back."

The kitchen gave them a real shock. It had been gleaming and sunny under Mrs. Dunn's rule. Now, it seemed crowded and dark. The walls were roughly whitewashed but the small windows did not let in much light; the beamed ceiling was hung with hams and bacon, which made it seem even lower than it was. The floor was brick, and there was a huge fireplace which took up all of one wall. A plump woman with a shining moon of a face under a white ruffled cap was stirring an iron pot which hung from a crane over the fire. She glanced up at them without any particular curiosity, and said, " 'Ee'll be the children Master Turner spoke on. Well, and good mornin' and do 'ee, boys, one run and get me a bucket o' water and t'others may fill the woodbox."

Joe and Possible groaned together. "No sink, no faucet, no refrigerator, no gas stove, no electricity," said Possible under his breath. "How can she manage?"

Danny took the bucket and soon found the well outside not far from the door, while the other two got armloads of wood from a lean-to beside the kitchen and filled the wooden box next to the fireplace. Then they all sat down on benches at the long table and fell upon their breakfast.

There was porridge which tasted like gritty oatmeal with honey over it, hot corn bread, thick slices of bacon very smokey from the fire, and cool buttermilk. The four ate like fiends, and by the time Professor Bullfinch, Mr. Turner, and Mr. Franklin came in, the boys were on their third helpings of bacon, and even Irene was still gobbling corn bread dipped in honey.

The Professor looked a little rumpled. The other two men, however, were neatly dressed in long coats, knee breeches, woolen stockings, and shoes with metal buckles. Danny looked hard at their hair, although he tried not to, and saw that they were both indeed wearing wigs: Mr. Turner's rather short and rounded in the back, and Mr. Franklin's fuller and longer. Both wigs were gray.

"Well, good morrow, good morrow," said Mr. Turner, rubbing his hands cheerfully. "I see our young friends have wasted little time this morning. Lost time is never found again, as our Poor Richard has written, eh, Ben?"

Mr. Franklin laughed. "You recall more of my work than I do, my dear Jonathan," he said.

"If the Professor gets the chronocycle working, though, that saying will be wrong," said Danny, mischievously.

Professor Bullfinch shot him a warning look, motioning toward the plump woman, who was bringing fresh bowls of porridge to the table. Mr. Turner saw the look and smiled.

"You've no need to concern yourself about our Nan, my dear Professor," he said. "She's been with me for too long to be surprised at anything. And she is discreet, as well. Nan, you'll have seen the new outbuilding in the back?"

"Aye, sir, I have," said Nan, putting the bowls on the table. "It do be in my way for feedin' the hens."

"Well, we'll have it away before long. Be sure you don't go into it, however."

"Not for a hundred pound, be sure of it," she replied. "More of your wild devil's work, without doubt. Will it be small beer or buttermilk this morning, sir?"

"Beer, please, Nan. And you, Professor? Will you try some of our brewing?"

"Not for breakfast, thanks. I'm afraid I'm not used to it."

"I didn't know you lived in Midston, Mr. Franklin," Irene said.

"No more he does, my child," said Mr. Turner. "He is about to set out on an inspection of his precious post offices, but before doing so came to spend a few days with me, as we are old drinking companions, to argue a bit and quarrel through the night, and so that he might tell me of his English visit last year."

"A delightful land, England," Mr. Franklin said. "I confess my thoughts have often turned to making my home there, although I cannot persuade my good Debby to cross the seas. Of all the enviable things England has, I envy it most its people. That pretty island, with scarce enough of it above water to keep one's shoes dry, enjoys more sensible, virtuous, and elegant minds in any neighborhood than we can collect in ranging a hundred leagues of our vast forests."

"Yet I have heard you speak ill of some of the English, Ben," Mr. Turner smiled.

"Oh—our good King's advisors, some of them, are no more than madmen. I think they must come to their senses before long. If not, I fear contentions in some of our provinces."

Joe pressed close to Danny, and said in his ear, "Gosh, he doesn't even seem to know about the American Revolution."

"How can he?" Danny whispered back. "It's twelve years off."

"I wish I'd studied more history," Irene said, also in a whisper. "I didn't know that Mr. Franklin had anything to do with the post office."

"Yes," Mr. Franklin was saying, "only Pitt showed intelligence during the late war. But now that that is over with, it may be they can devote more attention to our other affairs."

"What war is he talking about?" Possible asked, softly.

But Professor Bullfinch was already getting to his feet. "I hate to put an end to this pleasant conversation," he said, "but we simply must have a look at the chronocycle."

Mr. Franklin cleared his throat. "Ah—Jonathan and I—we'd count it an honor, sir," he said, "if we might be permitted to watch. I assure you, we should sit mum in a corner. . . . "

Irene began to giggle, and covered her face with her hands.

"I can't help it," she gasped, blushing furiously. "He—he sounds just like Danny does when he wants to watch an experiment. Oh, please forgive me, Mr. Franklin—"

"No offense, my little maid," said Mr. Franklin. "Indeed, I fear we are scarce better than children in the face of your Professor's science."

"Of course you may come," said the Professor. "Can we go out this way, through the kitchen?"

The laboratory was just as they had left it the night before. The Professor went at once to the control cabinet and began to unbolt its rear plate.

Joe, with his hands in his pockets, remarked, "You know, my Pop once worked for nearly an hour on a television set and then found that it just wasn't plugged in. Maybe that's what's wrong with this thing."

The Professor slowly straightened up and regarded Joe with surprise. "Brilliant youth!" he said. "You're right!"

"Do you mean it really is unplugged?" said Possible.

"In a way, yes," the Professor replied. "What an idiot I was not to think of it. You see, the time field is activated by a spark. The spark is furnished, as I told you, by a condenser. The condenser was completely discharged when we took that long jump back two hundred years. It was supposed to be recharged by direct current from an outside source. But of course, now that we're in the eighteenth century, there aren't any outside sources! All our power sources, both direct and alternating, are gone. Naturally, that's why our lights didn't work. And that's why the condenser isn't recharged."

Mr. Franklin and Mr. Turner were listening with awe.

Mr. Franklin said, "Bless my soul, Jonathan, do you *see?* The youngsters—why, they appear to know what he's talking about!"

Mr. Turner sighed. "We are mere infants, Ben."

"We must ask him some questions," said Mr. Franklin.

"We would scarce know how to begin," Mr. Turner said, wryly. "And he would hardly know how to begin to answer. Imagine yourself trying to explain to a savage Indian how your electrical fluid works—"

Danny whirled round. "Professor!" he exclaimed. "That's it."

He pointed at Mr. Franklin, who looked startled.

"I remember that much history," Danny went on. "Mr. Franklin's experiments with electricity. That's our answer!"

10
A Walk in
Yesterday

Mr. Franklin stared at the boy's flushed, eager face. "I am most gratified," he said, "if you think I can provide any answer to your problem. But I am afraid I understand nothing at all."

"Danny's quite right," said Professor Bullfinch. "You see, gentlemen, this apparatus of mine requires a spark of electricity to start its action. That spark is provided by what we call a condenser, or a capacitor— a way of storing up electricity. Doesn't that sound familiar to you, Mr. Franklin?"

"Why, of course. An electrical bottle!"

"Yes. You yourself called it a Leyden bottle, and we still call that early storage device a Leyden jar. Actually, it's a kind of battery—"

"Exactly the word I used! You remember, Jonathan, I wrote to Collinson nearly fifteen years ago about our making a battery of glass and leaden plates—?"

"Yes, sir, we think you may have made the very first storage battery," said the Professor. "Well, a good big Leyden jar would be enough for my purposes. Since Mr. Turner has also performed electrical experiments, perhaps he has one somewhere?"

"I have two enormous ones," Mr. Turner cried. "In my workshop. And the globes for charging them. I once made a spark nearly seven inches long. Let's go at once and find them."

His workshop was a longish room behind the parlor, which in Danny's time had become a library and music room, in which Professor Bullfinch kept his phonograph, sheet music, and the bull-fiddle on which he was an enthusiastic amateur performer. Now, it was filled with shelves, a high-fronted desk, a long table, and a bookcase. The children caught glimpses of strange instruments, some of which they recognized from their schoolbooks. There was an astrolabe, an armillary sphere which showed the positions of the planets, some scales, several magnifying lenses, and a brass telescope. Mr. Turner and Mr. Franklin pulled out two contraptions mounted on wooden stands and began blowing the dust off them. They consisted of glass globes mounted on axles, turned by wheels with handles on them, and connected to silvered glass jars with metal rods set in them.

"Don't look so bewildered," the Professor told the young people. "I'll explain it all later. Essentially, they're quite simple. You know that you can produce a spark by rubbing your feet on a thick carpet? Or even, sometimes, by brushing your hair? Well, these glass globes, when they're turned so that they rub against disks of sulphur or pieces of silk, produce electricity by friction in the same way. The Leyden jar collects the charge in its metal rod."

"Too bad we aren't having a good thunderstorm," Mr. Turner grunted, as he and Mr. Franklin lifted one of the stands. "We could gather all the electricity we wished."

"I'd say it was just as well," grinned the Professor. "You gentlemen never showed the proper respect for lightning. I'm astonished more of your friends weren't electrocuted.

Come on, boys, give us a hand to carry these things to the lab."

Mr. Franklin was muttering, "Electrocuted! A new word. Most interesting."

They soon had the equipment set up in the laboratory next to the chronocycle. The Professor set to work at once, turning the handle of one of the wheels so that the glass globe began spinning rapidly. Mr. Franklin seized the second handle.

"Uh—Professor," Danny said, timidly. "I've been thinking . . . "

"You'll have your chance at this work soon, Dan," the Professor puffed.

"It's not that. I mean—well—if we were on a boat, and it landed in a far country for just a very little while . . . "

He looked at Irene and the two Joes. They nodded enthusiastically.

"Oho! So that's it," said Professor Bullfinch. "You want to go ashore and explore, eh?" He stopped cranking and blinked at them through his spectacles. "I thought you didn't like the past, Dan."

Danny wriggled uncomfortably. "I just thought . . . "

"Thought it wasn't real? It might be real enough for you to get into trouble. Still want to go outside?"

"I thought you didn't like the past, Dan."

"Yes, sir!" said Danny.

"So do we," Irene said.

"You bet!" chorused the two Joes.

"I really see no harm in it, sir," said Mr. Franklin. "I can well believe they may be mad with curiosity. I am sure you, too, desire to see the young improve themselves by a wholesome exercise of the spirit of discovery. And while a man of your years and appearance might excite some talk in the village, I suppose children would attract little attention no matter how oddly dressed."

"I guess you're right," said the Professor. "But for heaven's sake, be careful, kids. And Danny—don't go charging off headlong into anything. I want you all here safely in an hour."

The young people ran into the fresh air as if they had been let out of a cage.

"Notice something?" Danny said. "It's so quiet. No cars, no trucks, and no airplanes, that's why."

"And the air smells so good," Irene said. "Funny—it's as if you could suddenly smell *everything*. Flowers, grass, the dust, wood smoke, all sorts of things you never notice at home."

They all had gotten used to speaking of their own time as "home."

Irene stopped at the kitchen door. "Wait for me," she begged. "I'll only be a sec."

She dashed into the house. It took a little longer than a second, but in a very short time she reappeared. The boys gaped at her. She was wearing a long, flowered skirt and a shawl pulled around her shoulders and pinned at the waist.

"Who are you supposed to be—Betsy Ross?" said Possible.

"I'm supposed to be a girl from somewhere around this year," Irene retorted. "It may not look very stylish, but it won't make people goggle at me the way my own short skirt and sweater might."

"Good idea," Danny said. "Where'd you get them? From Mrs. Nan?"

"Uh-huh. It was the first time I saw her look surprised, too—she fingered my sweater and looked it all over, and said, 'Lawks! Who'd 'a knitted that, now?' "

She gave so accurate an imitation of the plump woman that they all laughed.

They walked out into the dusty road, shyly keeping rather close together.

"Listen, let's head up toward Washington Avenue," Danny suggested. "We can see where the school is going to be, and look over toward the airport and the University."

The others agreed. They strolled slowly up what would one day be called Elm Street, and Irene pointed out a huge old elm with a rough log seat in front of it. "I'll bet that's why it came to be called Elm Street in the first place," she said. "Only that tree is standing where Mr. Parker's house is going to be."

"I wonder when they cut it down?" Danny said. "Look, there's a whipping post and some stocks behind the elm."

"The hills look just the same," Joe said. "There's old Sugarloaf sticking up above the trees."

Possible crossed the road and stood in front of the stocks. "This is where they put you when you don't do your homework, I guess," he said. "See, the top part lifts off and then you put your hands through the holes and they put the top bar back on and lock you in."

"Ugh! Don't try it," Joe said. "Suppose we couldn't get you out?"

A woman carrying two pails which hung from either end of a yoke that passed over her shoulders, walked by and greeted them politely.

"Strangers, be you?" she said.

"Yes, ma'am," said Irene, curtsying.

"Stopping with someone in t' town?"

"With Mr. Turner, ma'am," Danny said.

She looked him up and down and stared at the two Joes. "My dears," she said, "where did you ever get such rigs?"

"We're—we're from the far north, ma'am," Danny said. "All the kids—I mean, all the children dress like this there."

"Think o' that. And be they all Frenchies up there?"

"Oh, no. We're Americans, just like you."

She smiled. "Not like me, love. I be English, and bonded to Squire Middes."

She nodded a good-by, and went off.

"What did she mean, 'bonded'?" Joe asked. "And who's Squire Middes?"

"Oh!" Irene said. "I'll bet I know. He's the man Midston is named after. Remember how Mr. Turner pronounced it? *Middestown*. Golly, I can hardly wait to get home. I want to look it up in the library and see if I'm right."

Danny was trying to remember his history. "Bonded," he said, "means—anyway, I think it means—that this squire paid her passage over here and she has to work for him until the price is paid off. It's something rather like slavery, I think."

"Gee, did they have slaves up here? I thought that was only in the South," said Joe.

"No, they had slaves all over, and both white and black people, too. Even George Washington owned slaves," Danny replied.

"I wonder if old Mrs. Nan is Mr. Turner's slave," Joe said. "Kind of a depressing thought, isn't it?"

They walked a little further, past a narrow shady lane with four or five houses set along it. There was a small open field to their left, and half a dozen children were playing some sort of ball game in it. The four stopped to watch. One boy was standing in front of a three-legged stool with a flat paddle in his hands, while another boy threw a ball toward him, using a strange kind of over-hand toss. The first boy swung his paddle and hit the ball; one of the girls ran forward and caught it.

"Good catch!" Joe said. "A pop fly."

"Go on, it was a foul," Possible objected.

The children—two of them were girls—had stopped their game and came slowly toward the four friends.

"Hi," Danny said, feeling a little nervous.

The children looked at each other and then at the newcomers.

"High? What's high?" said the boy with the paddle. "Is it a joke?"

"No, I meant how are you?" Danny said. "How-are-you—h'are ya—hi. See?"

"Oh. Hi. Where do you come from?"

"We're from a long way off. Just visiting," Irene said.

"Them two's just alike," said the smallest boy, pointing at Joe and Possible. "Why?"

"We're twins," said Joe.

There was silence for a moment as the children studied each other. The girls were dressed like the women of the time, with longish skirts, while the boys wore a sort of short-legged overall. They were all barefoot.

At last Joe said, "What's that game you were playing?"

"Stool ball. Or cricket, we calls it some-times, 'cos the stool's a cricket, you know," said the biggest boy. "Don't you know that?"

"Nope. All we know are baseball, foot-ball, basketball, and things like that."

"We play football," said the biggest boy. "Only 'ee can't play it barefoot, so we plays it in winter when we wear our boots. Where'd 'ee get them cloth shoes?"

The four looked down at their sneakers. "Why—everybody wears 'em where we come from," Danny said.

"And where's that?" asked one of the girls.

Joe sighed. "Now we're back where we started," he said. "We're from East Pumper-nickel, Maine. Okay?"

"Okay? I know where the province of Maine is," said the biggest boy, "for I've an uncle living there. But I don't know where Okay is."

"Say, how about teaching us that stoolball game?" Possible put in, quickly, to change the subject.

"All right, come along," said the boy with the paddle. He held it out to Possible. "You can bat."

"Oh, is that what it is?" Possible said. "I thought you had lost your canoe."

Irene was already deep in conversation

with the two girls. "You play without us," she called. "I'm just sort of asking them about clothes and things."

"I don't want to play either," Danny said. "I'm going to walk up to the end of the road."

Joe shrugged. "I'll come with you. That's the nice thing about there being two of me. One can go play, and the other one can keep on walking. Hey, Possible!"

"What?"

"Stay right here, will you, so we can pick you up later."

"Okay."

Danny and Joe set off again. "You know, it's all different from what I'd have thought, from the history books," Joe mused.

"What do you mean?"

"Why, when you read the history books you get the idea that people just stood around listening to speeches, and that it would all be sort of quaint and they'd be talking about George Washington and Patrick Henry, and—and so on. Instead it's just like a day anywhere, people are going about their business—there's a woman hanging up her wash in her yard, and there's a guy 'way over there in that field ploughing with a horse. It doesn't look so quaint or funny now that we've seen it and gotten used to it. It just looks natural. I guess nobody here realizes that they're supposed to be our historic past."

Danny laughed. "I know how you feel," he said. "It's like when we saw that man in buckskins and a coonskin cap, this morning, and thought he must be Kit Carson, or Daniel Boone. But he was really just an ordinary guy going off on a hunt, somebody nobody ever heard of—Mr. Jones, of Midston."

He stuck his hands deep in his pockets. "When you come right down to it," he said, "I suppose in our own time *we're* history, too. We must be living in history every day. And maybe two hundred years from our time, kids will read in their history books about our quaint old costumes, and our politics and speeches, and think about *us* as the historic past."

Joe nodded. "I guess the trouble is we study history as names and dates, and then it doesn't seem to be about real people. I suppose history is just every day for a long time, a couple of thousand years or more. And I guess it's things changing every day, so that you don't even notice them unless you happen to get a long way off from them. . . ."

Danny interrupted. "Talking about changes—look, Joe. That's where the garage and service station used to stand. Isn't it?"

They had come to a crossroad, not much more than another dirt track winding away through the trees. A large house stood on the corner with a signboard on a post in front of it. There was a rearing lion in dark red painted on the faded gilt of the board. A couple of horses were tied to a rail, and there were a bench and a trestle table beside the door.

"What do you mean, 'used to stand'?" Joe snorted. "The garage won't even be thought of for a hundred and fifty years."

Danny shaded his eyes and squinted along the crossrod. "This must be Washington Avenue," he said. "I wonder what they call it now? And this building—I'll bet it's a tavern or an inn. Let's look inside."

"Maybe they don't allow kids in there," Joe said, uneasily.

"Oh, come on. All they can do is throw us out."

Danny went to the door, took a breath, and stepped inside, and after an instant's hesitation, Joe followed.

11
The Red Lion Inn

The room was lighted by three windows with tiny, diamond-shaped leaded panes and at first the boys could barely make anything out. There was a strong yeasty smell. As their eyes grew accustomed to the dimness, they saw a counter with a couple of small barrels on a shelf behind it, a few round tables and one long, narrow one, a couple of benches, some stools, and a pair of high-backed settles on either side of the fireplace.

Then a man loomed up before them. He was in shirt sleeves and had a dirty apron tied around his waist. He wore an untidy-looking wig which sat crooked on his head.

"Now, then," he said. "No nonsense.

Can't have no boys tramping about here. What are you after?"

"We just wanted to look around," Danny said. "Is this an inn?"

"The Red Lion," said the man. "All mine, Jeremy Tucker, fair and square as ever was." He stooped to squint at them. "Who are you? You aren't no local younkers."

"No, sir," said Danny.

A voice from one of the settles, a rasping, sandpapery sort of voice, said, "Pair o' gypsies, I'll be bound, Jeremy. Let's 'ave a look at 'em."

A tall, skinny man stood up. He had been concealed by the shadows of the settle. He had a short clay pipe in his mouth, a long blue coat laced with very tarnished silver, a wig with a long pigtail that hung down his back, muddy boots, and a batttered three-cornered hat cocked down over his eyes. He came forward with his hands behind his back, and grinned crookedly at the boys.

"My, my, ain't we the lovely, tarry lads," he growled, pointing at Joe's red and white striped shirt. "Wearin' a sailor's shirt, eh? And canvas slops as well. What ship ye off, mates?"

"We're—we're not from any ship," Danny said, realizing that the man had mistaken their dungarees for sailors' clothing. "We're staying with Mr. Turner."

"Think o' that, now. *Stayin'* with 'im? 'E'd be your grandpapa, no doubt?"

"No, he's no relation."

"Ah?" The man inspected them more closely, and then winked at the innkeeper. "And where might you be from, me little pals?"

Joe said, "Oh, we're from a long way off. Nowhere around here."

"Is that right, now?"

The man suddenly reached out a long arm and seized Joe by the shoulder. "Come on, me young imperence. You're indentured, now, ain't you?"

Joe wriggled, but the man's fingers were like steel claws. "I—I don't know," he gasped. "I am if I'm supposed to be."

"Ha! What about it, Jeremy? Couple o' runaways, eh? Stayin' with Mr. Turner— that's a lark."

"Here! You let him go," Danny said, fiercely. "I'll call a cop. You can't do that."

"You cop *'im,* Jeremy," the man snapped.

"Why, I don't know—" the innkeeper began.

That gave Danny his chance. He rushed forward and butted the innkeeper in the

Danny butted the innkeeper in the stomach.

stomach. The man said, "Oof!" and staggered back, crashing into a chair. Danny flew at the other fellow and hit at him with all his might.

The man grabbed his jacket collar. "Run, Joe!" Danny yelled. He broke loose, hearing his collar rip, and made for the door.

He burst into the street and stood there, panting. But to his horror, Joe wasn't with him. Instead, the innkeeper appeared at the doorway, clutching his stomach, red-faced and angry. He started for Danny and the boy ran. He dodged behind the nearest house, darted across a stubble field, and dropped sobbing for breath at the foot of a big tree.

The innkeeper had not followed him. Dan got up after a moment and walked back to the road. He could see the doorway of the inn: it was closed and no one was in sight. He began trotting back down the road.

Possible was still in the field with the boys, swinging the bat and calling for a "nice, low, fast one that I can knock out of the ball park." Irene was sitting by the roadside with the two girls.

She took one look at Dan's face, and said, "What's wrong?"

"Joe," Danny gulped. "He's been kidnapped."

Irene sprang to her feet. Danny put his hands to his mouth and yelled, "Possible! On the double! Come on—drop the game."

Possible came jogging over to them. "Just when I was getting good," he said. "What's up? Where's Joe?"

Danny took him by the arm and tried to smile at the other children. "We've got to go now, kids," he said. "Thanks for being so nice. We'll see you again some time."

He caught Irene's hand and walked both his friends rapidly back up the road before the village youngsters could ask any questions.

"Joe's been taken prisoner by two men," he said, as they walked. "One of them's the innkeeper and the other is some kind of crook. They thought we were runaways, maybe from some ship. We've got to get him back."

"But how? Why not just get the Professor and Mr. Turner and Mr. Franklin?" said Possible. "Mr. Franklin—that's it! He's an important man. He could do something."

"First, let's find out what's happening," said Danny. "It's my fault. We should never have gone into that inn. I've got to find out what they've done with Joe."

They had come in sight of the Red Lion.

The door was still shut and the place silent.

Danny whispered, "I'm going to snoop around. Maybe I can hear something. You two wait here."

He didn't stop for an answer but darted away, bent over nearly double, to the corner of the inn. Possible and Irene watched him slip along the side of the building and vanish in the rear.

They waited, biting their lips nervously, for what seemed to them a very long time. At last, Irene said, "I can't stand this. You run back to the house and get Mr. Franklin. I'm going to march right in there and find out what's going on."

"Nothing doing," said Possible. "You go get Mr. Franklin. I'll go in and—and—"

"And what?"

"I don't know. Maybe we could set fire to the place?"

Fortunately, Danny appeared just then. He slipped back to join them, his sneakers making no sound in the dust.

"I know where he is," he said. "They've got him shut up in a closet next to the bar. I found an open window on the other side of the house, and listened under it. I could hear them talking. The innkeeper kept saying he wasn't sure they should get mixed up in anything like this, but the other fellow said there was no doubt Joe and I were runaways and had just mentioned staying with Mr. Turner out of desperation. He said maybe we heard the name somewhere. He said it didn't matter if I'd got off, and he'd take Joe with him tied up on his other horse and make for the coast. He said he was sure he could either find his owner, or sell him to a sea captain and they'd split the money."

"Sell him?" Irene squealed. "He can't do that. Joe's an American citizen."

"That's what he said," Danny answered. "And if he said so, I'll bet he can do it. Now listen, I've thought it all out. This is what we'll do. . . . "

Meantime, inside the inn, Jeremy Tucker had just filled two wooden tankards with ale. He gave one to his rascally friend, Toddy Steward, and they were lifting them to their lips when there came a loud knock at the door.

"Ah, it's time I opened up again," Tucker said, putting down his drink. He pulled open the door and stood petrified with amazement.

There before his eyes was the very boy he and Steward thought they had safely shut up in the cupboard. There was no mistaking that long face, black hair, and especially the red and white striped shirt.

"Yaah!" said the boy, sticking out his tongue and crossing his eyes. "Thought you had me, didn't you?"

Tucker snatched at him, but the boy danced away. Steward rushed for the door, spilling beer over everything. He ran out into the street with Tucker right behind him.

The moment they were through the door, Irene darted inside. She went to the cupboard beside the bar and shot back the bolt. Joe was leaning limply against a shelf.

"Come on!" she cried. "Don't ask questions."

They both ran out of the inn. Possible had vanished, and the innkeeper and his friend lay sprawled in the ditch on the other side of the road.

Danny had been waiting for them. As they chased Possible across the road, Danny had thrown himself from behind a tree in a flying tackle at Steward's legs. The man had tripped over him and fallen headlong. Dan had rolled and the innkeeper, trying to jump over him and unable to stop, had crashed down on top of Steward.

Danny leaped up and took off like the wind. Irene and Joe were at his heels. Possible joined them and they ducked to one side between a house and a barn. Chickens scattered away squawking. They vaulted a low rail fence, ran through a grove of trees, around another house, and found themselves in the open place where the stocks and the old elm tree stood. They got behind the tree and peeped cautiously up the road. In the distance, they could see the innkeeper looking about, but there was no sign of his friend.

"It doesn't matter if they do see us, now," Danny panted. "It's only a few steps. Let's go!"

They shot across the road and into the shadow of a lilac hedge. A minute later, they were in Mr. Turner's yard. They ran to the laboratory door and plunged through it, exhausted.

Professor Bullfinch was sitting quietly on the bench, smoking his pipe between Mr. Turner and Mr. Franklin.

"See there," he said mildly, "how responsible these young people are, gentlemen. I told them to come back in an hour, and they've run all the way so as not to be late."

12
An Oversight

"Is the spark ready?" Danny said, when he could catch his breath.

"Why, yes," said the Professor. "We've just this minute finished charging the two Leyden jars."

"Then let's get going," Danny urged.

"Oh, there really isn't that much hurry," said the Professor. "I was just trying to explain molecular theory to Mr. Turner and Mr. Franklin—"

"And finding it exceedingly hard going," chuckled Mr. Franklin. "I'm afraid we simply do not have the words, or the background, to understand your new philosophy. In any case, I am not a scientist but a poor businessman who is concerned with matters of statecraft."

"But, listen!" said Danny. "There's been some trouble."

"I am greatly tempted to stay on for a few days," the Professor said. "Or a few weeks, for that matter, since we can return to our own—What did you say?" He stared at Danny. "What kind of trouble?"

"Some men tried to kidnap us. I got away, but they grabbed Joe, but then Irene and Possible and I got him back and we dumped them in the ditch and ran and ran and I think we got away from them but they might come looking for us."

He stopped for lack of breath. Professor Bullfinch exchanged glances with the others; they were looking very perplexed and disturbed.

"What men were these?" Mr. Franklin said.

"One was the man who owns the Red Lion Inn, and the other was a tall, thin fellow with a raspy voice."

"Toddy Steward. I know him," said Mr. Turner, grimly. "A worthless stick, ran off from England for some misdeed and came hither. He comes and goes in Middestown, and has been suspected of dirty affairs although naught has been proved upon him, but he is the leader of several rascally fellows in the village. As for Jeremy Tucker, he is not above wickedness, I fear, for there has been talk of smuggled goods passing through his hands."

"But why did they try to seize you?" Mr. Franklin asked.

"First, they thought we were from some ship, because of our clothes. Then they said we were runaways, and that fellow Toddy asked Joe if he was—what was it, Joe?"

"I think he asked me if I was insured," said Joe.

"Insured?" Mr. Franklin wrinkled his forehead. Then his face cleared. "Indentured? Did he ask if you were indentured?"

"Yes, that's it. I didn't know what it meant, and I figured that maybe it was something I was supposed to be, so I said I guessed I was."

Mr. Franklin uttered a laugh, and then looked very serious.

Mr. Turner said, "To be indentured, my boy, is to be bound to someone for a term of work. They thought you were a banded servant, someone's runaway boy. As such, if they could find your master they could claim a reward, or, failing that, they could sell you to some ship's captain, let us say, as a cabin boy."

"This is very grave," said Mr. Franklin. "For if you could not prove that you were indeed a freeman, you might be treated as a slave. But that is not the worst of it, Jonathan," he went on, turning to his friend. "If this rogue, Toddy Steward, should come prowling after his runaways and find this building, we might have awkward questions to answer."

"Yes, and what about me?" said the Professor. "I might have a certain amount of difficulty answering a great many questions."

He got up, cramming his pipe into his pocket. "It's too bad you young people got into that mess," he said, "but on the other hand, perhaps it's just as well. You might have had trouble getting me to go home, otherwise."

The other two men had risen as well, and Mr. Franklin said, "It has been an honor and a privilege, sir, to have met you and conversed with you. I find it hard, already, to believe that you are indeed from another age. And I suspect we will find it equally hard, when you are gone, not to think this was all some dream, some fantastical bewitchment that came and passed in a breath."

There came a knocking at the lab door, and they all jumped. It was Mr. Turner's housekeeper, Nan, motioning at them through the glass pane. The Professor opened the door.

"I do beg pardon, sir," she said, dropping a sketchy curtsy, "but there's a—I won't say gen'leman, for that tattered, thieving, lantern-jawed ruffian ain't worth the word—a person to see Master Turner."

"Toddy Steward, eh?" said Mr. Turner. And when she nodded, he went on, "He's come quicker than we expected."

"I'm afraid we told him we were visiting you, sir," Danny said.

"Hm! Then we must say farewell to you all," said Mr. Turner. "Ben, I'll be obliged if you'll step inside with me. We will keep the villain entertained whilst they get away. If he should take it into his head to pry or poke about the place, let him find nothing but trouble."

He stepped forward and shook the Professor's hand. "God bless you, sir," he said, "and send you safe home."

Mr. Franklin shook hands with them all, too. "Good-by to you, and God speed," he smiled.

Irene whipped off the skirt and shawl and

returned them to Nan, who kissed her on the cheek and whispered, "I don't know where you're goin', duck, but 'ave a good trip."

When they had all gone, the Professor turned to the chronocycle. He reached for the switches. And then he paused, with his hand in mid-air.

"Goodness gracious!" he said. "There's one thing I had completely forgotten."

"What is it?" said Irene. "Not us—we're all here."

The Professor's face had become very pale. "I hadn't thought how to get us back to the right day of our own, exact time," he said.

13
The Long Count

"Do you mean there's still something wrong with the machine?" Irene asked.

"Not at all," replied Professor Bullfinch. "But if I start the chronocycle, I haven't any way of knowing precisely when to stop it so that we will return to the day we left."

"What about the computer?" Danny said.

"All it does is calculate probabilities in the past or future. But I can't set it for a particular day—Saturday, April 27, 1963—and have it stop there, and at noon. I can only set the power so that it governs the strength of the field." The Professor took out his pipe and began turning it over and over between his hands rather helplessly.

"Can't you just—mm—reverse the chronocycle?" said Joe.

"It's not like an automobile, Joe," the Professor replied. "In the first place, we didn't come here from our own day, if you remember. We left from a possible Tuesday in the future when you and Dan had your somewhat panicky struggle, and started the machine by accident. We have to have some fairly accurate way of calculating our distance back to our own day so that I'll know when to stop. Otherwise, we might go jumping all over time!"

"Then we're cooked," said Possible. "We'll have to stay here forever. Those men will catch us and sell us to somebody—they'll work us like slaves—they won't feed us—I'll starve! I'll waste away to a shadow and vanish—and I won't even know whether I'm really me or just a possibility."

He clutched at Joe. "Let's run off and join the Indians," he groaned. "At least they'll feed us."

Danny began to laugh.

"It's no laughing matter," Joe said, mournfully. "He's right."

"I'm not laughing at that," said Danny. "I'm laughing because we've all forgotten that we *do* have a—a kind of mileage meter on the chronocycle. He just reminded me of it when he said, 'waste away to a shadow.' Joe, don't you remember my shadow measuring?"

"Shadow——? Oh, yes." Joe scratched his head. "What's that got to do with it?"

"A two-foot stick throws a three-foot shadow, so a twenty-foot house throws a thirty-foot shadow," Danny said. "Professor—look at the screen on the control board. Isn't there a line on it?"

Professor Bullfinch leaned forward. "Of course!" he said. "Just as there was that first time."

The others looked too, and Irene said, "This one runs halfway across the screen and stops."

"Sure!" Danny crowed. "It shows how far we've come. It ends on the day we arrived. Couldn't it be a kind of shadow of how far we've moved in time? Remember, the first line had three peaks. And we moved three days. Each peak must represent a day."

"Hmm." The Professor cradled his chin in his hand. "We don't know that for certain."

"No, but it's worth taking a chance on. Isn't it, Professor?" said Irene.

Danny was already busily figuring on a

piece of paper. "Two hundred years would make 73,000 days—or peaks," he said.

"Wait a minute," Irene put in. "You've forgotten Leap Year."

"Leave it to a girl to remember that," grinned Dan.

"Correct," said the Professor. "Seventy-three thousand and fifty days—no, forty-nine, because we've been here one day." He stood for a moment in thought, and then made up his mind. "Very well. I'll start the chronocycle. Dan, you and Irene will count the peaks in the line as they appear. You'd better take it in turn or you'll wear out—count a thousand each. When you get to 73,049, I'll go a sixteenth of an inch further so we'll land at noon, since my experiment began a bit before that, and then I'll stop the machine."

He put a hand on the shoulder of each. "It's going to be a tough job, counting those peaks," he said. "And we mustn't make a mistake."

"Don't worry, Professor," Danny said earnestly. "We won't fail. Will we, Irene?"

Irene was pale, but she said, "No, we won't," trying her best to sound confident.

Joe said, sourly, "I'm not sure I want to

go. Trouble, trouble! Suppose the whole thing blows up?"

"I hardly think that will happen, Joe," said the Professor. "We know, now, that the chronocycle works, and we know how it works. We're taking a chance that these peaks are twenty-four hour intervals. The only problem is counting the days correctly so that we don't land in the middle of the Civil War, or in some distant future. Do you and Possible want to take turns at counting?"

"We'd better not," said Joe, with a sigh. "Arithmetic's our worst subject. We'll just have to trust you three."

Possible pulled at his sleeve. "As long as there's nothing else we can do," he said, "sit down and let's make up a poem. It'll keep our minds off anything going wrong."

"Okay," said Joe. "What's a good rhyme for 'chronocycle'?"

"How about 'once up*on* a cycle'?" Possible muttered, holding his head between his hands.

The Professor turned from them. "All right, stand by," he said. "Here we go."

Once again, came the loud snap, and the dark fog settled over them. Once again, the tangle of rods and coils glowed with an unnatural light, a firefly glimmering that spread out, around and *through* them. Danny was already counting monotonously and steadily: ". . . five, six, seven, eight, nine . . ." Irene, waiting for her turn, could not help echoing him in a faint whisper.

The black line unrolled swiftly. When he neared the end of his thousand, Dan touched the peaks with the point of a pencil so that Irene could pick up the count. And she began: "One thousand . . . and one . . . and two . . ."

Their throats and lips grew dry. It seemed to them that they had been counting forever as if in a nightmare. And still they kept sternly at it, pattering out the numbers coolly and rapidly. It was the hardest job either of them had ever done, harder than washing windows or chopping wood, harder than any homework, harder than getting up on a winter morning to go to school, or making yourself go to bed on a balmy summer night.

". . . forty-one thousand . . . and one . . . and two . . . and three . . ."

Irene's eyes watered, and she had to blink. Had she missed one? She bit her lip and went on counting, grimly putting all thought out of her mind.

". . . eight nine nine, fifty thousand nine hundred . . . and one . . ."

It was the hardest job they had ever done.

Steadily, the peaks moved on. The children counted as if they had become parts of the machine.

Irene's turn, and her voice rose a trifle. "Seven-two thousand, nine nine eight . . . nine nine nine . . . seventy-three thousand!"

The tension in the room was almost unbearable. Danny was croaking out the numbers, now. Irene, all else forgotten, counted with him. ". . . thirty-nine . . . forty . . ."

The Professor's hand was on the switch.

"—forty-six, forty-seven, forty-eight, *forty-nine!*"

"And a half," said the Professor. He slammed down the switch.

There was silence. The glow faded, and slowly the room filled with ordinary daylight.

Irene, blinking, said hoarsely. "Did it work? Are we back?"

Danny was holding his hands over his eyes. "I hope I never have to do anything like that again," he said.

"Oh, dear," said Irene. "The worst of it is, I don't know whether I missed one or not."

"I'll find out right now," said the Professor. "You all sit tight."

He pulled open the inner door, and there was the old familiar hallway once again. He hurried out, while the four young people simply stared at each other, unable to say a word. Where were they now? In some unimaginable future? Or in another past?

But when the Professor returned, they could tell by his bright, joyful expression that all was well.

"I looked at the kitchen calendar and the wall clock," he said. "It's Saturday—and ten minutes past noon. And Mrs. Dunn didn't even know we'd been gone. She told me that lunch would be ready in five minutes."

He began to laugh with relief, and the young people joined in.

"Danny—Irene," he said, throwing his arms around their shoulders and hugging them both. "You deserve a medal—two medals—six medals! I don't think I could have done that job."

"Saturday noon," said Joe, in a hushed voice. "And it was, say, about eleven-thirty when the Professor started the experiment. All those things that happened to us—why, they only took a little over a half-hour!"

"Did they?" said the Professor. "They only took half an hour of *this* time. There were two different times—this time, marked by our kitchen clock, and another time during which we went gallivanting around in the past and the future. And even there, there were differences. For instance, it seemed to take us much longer to return to this time than it did to go into the past. It will need a lot of study.

"And that reminds me," he added, "we've got one more task to do before lunch."

"Ah," said Possible, "you want to listen to our poem."

"No. I want to send Possible back to his own time," said the Professor. "He can't stay here."

"But how?" asked Joe.

"Quite simple. Now that we're back, we have our power again. And we know how to gauge distance. I'll take him. Danny, Irene, and Joe, you go along. I'll whiz Possible back to noon on Tuesday, chase him out of laboratory, and come back."

"Say, you know, that reminds me," Joe said. "I've been meaning to ask—how can he be real? He'd have been in school on Tuesday."

"But there wasn't any school because of a teacher's convention," Possible said. "Don't you remember?"

"Huh? Remember? How can I remember next Tuesday?" Joe said, dazedly.

"Professor—I don't think you should do it," said Danny, in a worried voice. "After all, we don't know for certain that *that* Tuesday is the *real* Tuesday. You might get stuck there and never get back."

"I won't be stuck, Dan. I'm following the same pattern of probability I followed the first time. Wherever—or whenever—that Tuesday is, it'll be the same one Possible first came from. Off with you, now!"

"But our poem!" cried Joe. "I may never see him—me—again. Don't you want to hear our poem?"

"Two minutes, then," the Professor said, firmly. "Can you recite it in two minutes?"

"You ought to have more respect for art," Joe said, drawing himself up.

"All right, three minutes. Any longer, and

we'll have Mrs. Dunn in here to see what's become of us, and what do you think she'll say if she finds two Joes?"

"Mom wouldn't care," Danny said. "She once told me that if she could put up with my inventions, nothing would surprise her any more."

"Nevertheless, I'd rather break the news to her in my own way," said the Professor. "Three minutes."

Joe cleared his throat and so did Possible. They put their arms around each other, and, speaking in chorus, began:

If I could go wherever I liked
In yesterday or tomorrow,
I'd travel back to a happy time
Where there was no gloom or sorrow.
When nobody yet had thought of school,
And there wasn't a word like "no,"
And every summer was clear and bright
And every winter had snow.
When nobody worked and everyone played
And candy was ten for a penny,
And nobody needed to take a bath
'Cause they hadn't invented any.
Well, I'd want to take everyone back with me
If I found that time somehow,
And then it wouldn't be "way back then,"
It would just be "here and now."

Everyone applauded, and Irene said, "That's a very *Joe* poem, I think. Especially the part about nobody needing to take a bath."

"That's a very high compliment, I guess," said Joe. "Isn't it? Or is it?"

"No more, now," Professor Bullfinch laughed. "Out of the room, you three. And shut the door. And *please*—"

"I know," Danny sighed. "No lurking around. Okay. So long, Possible. Good luck."

"But how will we ever know whether he got back—and whether he was really me— and whether it really was *our* Tuesday?" said Joe.

"I'm afraid," said the Professor, ushering them out of the laboratory, "that's something we will probably never be able to answer."

14
Joe Possible

The Professor had returned safely. He had been unable to tell them anything further about Possible other than that he had left the laboratory. The weekend had passed, and Monday had come and gone with its history test. On Tuesday, at noon, Danny, Irene, Mrs. Dunn, and the Professor were seated around the kitchen table, waiting for Joe who had been invited to have lunch with them.

"And it looks as though that possible Tuesday really *was* today," said Danny. "Because there was a teacher's convention and no school, just as Possible said."

"It's too bad you never thought to ask him about your history test," said Mrs. Dunn, who had heard the whole story soon after their return. "That might have helped you decide. If he took a history test on Monday, as you did—"

"Yes, Mom, but you know we were all so busy and confused that there were lots of things we never thought of," said Danny.

Mrs. Dunn nodded. "I can imagine," she said. "Going back to the eighteenth century. It's confusing enough being in *this* century! It's a good thing I didn't know where you were."

"But we were right here in this house most of the time," said Danny.

Mrs. Dunn looked a bit muddled. "I—I suppose that's so," she said.

"Anyway, the trip certainly made us study our history," Irene said, with her chin on her hands. "We won't get our marks until tomorrow, but I think we did well. And I found out that Squire Middes really was the man who founded Midston, in 1739. And in 1763, Mr. Franklin—we should have called him Doctor Franklin, you know, because he got a degree from Oxford the year before we met him—well, he was Deputy Postmaster General and he made a trip of inspection to all the post offices, starting in Virginia. He had just arranged for a better mail delivery, with the post traveling night and day so as to save time. If we'd come a little later, he'd have been in Virginia instead of visiting Mr. Turner."

"Yes, and that war he was talking about," said Danny, "was the war between England and France in which the French got the Indians to help them fight. It ended in February of 1763."

Professor Bullfinch glanced up at the clock. "Where on earth can Joe be?" he said. "I must get back to work. I've got a tremendous amount of research to do."

"Well, you needn't wait any longer," said Mrs. Dunn, getting up. "I'll give you your lunch—"

But at that moment, Joe appeared in the doorway.

"Where were you?" Danny asked. "You were supposed to be here before twelve, and it's nearly twenty after. You aren't usually late for food."

Joe had a very odd look on his face. He came into the room, stared around him, and slowly sat down at the table.

"I don't know how to tell you this," he said, and stopped.

"Speak!" said Irene. "What is it?"

"It's like this," Joe said. "I came over here

at a quarter to twelve. I was about to come in the front door, and then I suddenly thought, 'I wonder if they're in the lab?' So I went around to the back and walked into the laboratory——"

"We weren't there," said Danny. "We were already in the kitchen because Irene had just come over."

"That's the trouble," said Joe. "You *were* there, you and the Professor and Irene and somebody else. I said, 'Hi. What are you all doing in here?' And Danny, you said, 'What are *we* doing?' And then you started goggling at me like a goldfish—and then suddenly I realized that that other guy was me!"

"What? Why, that's exactly how it all happened the first time!" Irene spluttered.

"It *was* the first time," Joe said. "Everything happened just the way I remembered it was going to. We went back to the past, and met Mr. Franklin and Mr. Turner, and I got caught by that man in the Red Lion, and we escaped, and we came home, and the Professor took me back to the lab, and I went out the back door and—and here I am."

He put his hands to his head, and laughed hollowly. "How about that?" he said. "Am I going crazy? Or what?"

"Not at all, Joe," said the Professor calmly. "It only proves that you were really Possible all the time."

"But how could he be?" Irene gasped.

"Why not?" said the Professor. "We went to a possible Tuesday in which Joe walked into the laboratory. And sure enough, in he walked. Then we lived through the days between Saturday and Tuesday. Tuesday became the actual day—today—on which Joe walked into the laboratory. He's the same boy; they were just two different times."

"But what about us?" said Danny. "When he was walking into the lab that first time, were we sitting out here in the kitchen?"

"Possibly," aiswered the Professor, with a grin.

"But—Joe!" said Danny. "How did it feel as it was all happening again? Did you know everything that was coming?"

"It was like being in a dream, and watching yourself," Joe answered. "I could hear myself talking and see myself moving around, and I knew just how everything was going to happen but I couldn't change any of it. Even when we were in the Red Lion, I knew that man was going to grab me, and I knew what 'indentured' meant, but I couldn't keep from saying what I said, and I couldn't keep from being grabbed."